His Burdens...

When it comes to creating architecture, building businesses, positively impacting the world, and influencing the nations of the world, this man is rivaled by none. Success and his name are synonymous, yet when it comes to interpersonal relationships throughout life... from family... to lovers to friends, he became the antonym of success.

Over the course of five years, he begins constructing a sustainable dream island with an absolute paradise of infinite possibilities. After its completion, his presence slowly fades away from the outside world, and he travels to this island... untraceable... unaccompanied by anyone.

This book holds the letters, poems, and recounts of his life that he specially delivered to each of the 26 people he has ever truly loved in his life... Welcome To "His Burdens..."

By: Jeremiah Pouncy

Table Of Contents

<u>Author's Note</u>

The juxtaposition between a gift and a burden is always a concept that has fascinated me.

Who is to say my blessing is a gift... that unbeknownst to you, it is a burden...

Who is to say that my weakness is a burden... that unbeknownst to you, it is the fuel for my greatest gift...

So, you can read one story and get the picture, but if you read all, you will understand the masterpiece.

Map the intricate web of this man's life, and think about the crossroads of gifts and burdens in your life.

His
Burden Of
Adaptability

Queen Ocean

To be the burden

To know a burden
To know how heavy a load things can be
To know how they can affect a person
To know how to deal with a burden

To see a burden
To see what damage it can inflict
To see what unbearable weight drags behind
To see what immense dream can be crushed

To be a burden
To be the creator of turmoil in a life
To be the reason a family has a strife
To be the reason another life has no light

To be the burden
To know a burden
To see a burden
To be a burden
And above all else
Try your hardest not
To be THE burden
The burden to all but you
Yet you are THE burden
The burden to none but you

Opening

The beach's golden sand that has been weathered down by calm yet powerful waves is the perfect complement to the beauty of the clear, blue ocean. The sand and water live in excellent unison as if singing a song; this is where Queen and Jared Ocean seemingly belong.

...

It's 88 degrees outside, with the sun shining as bright as it can, unaccompanied by a single cloud in the sky. Underneath these clear blue skies lies a beautiful dark-skinned woman with eyes that glitter in the sun like gold.

She lays atop her dark purple beach towel as her husband sits atop his lawn chair, which holds precious memories of a broken family. Sweat drops slowly roll down each side of her face as the bright star from above continues to beam against her outstretched back.

And lying beside her is a small cardboard box she brought outside when the happily married couple first went out to the beach.

opens box

Looking down into her freshly opened cardboard box, she sees a book. A perfect-sized book... not too big... not too small. Not extremely daunting nor underwhelming. She sees the same book you're reading right now lying perfectly inside the small cardboard box she just opened. Gazing at the cover of this book, she reads, "His Burden Of Adaptability."

"You better not lose track of time and get sunburnt while you're reading that book, Queen," Jared says to her as he sits upon his dark blue chair under his matching umbrella.

"I won't, love," Queen says as she and her husband exchange smiles.

"I can't even say anything against that with you and your beautifully melanated skin," her husband says as he chuckles. "Well, what book did you order?"

"I don't remember ordering a book, nor do I know of any event that would compel someone to send me a book," she replies with a confused look. "I don't know why anyone would send me anything, to be completely honest with you."

"Do you think it could be from one of your friends in your book club," he asks inquiringly.

"No, I don't think so. We are still reading that incredible book, *Awakening of The End*, by Jeremiah Pouncy," she replies.

"Hmmm... well, maybe it was just a gift from somebody that wanted to say hello after a long time," he says back to Queen. He feels a gentle breeze blow upon his milk chocolate-toned skin as he utters these very words.

As the happily married couple, the wonderful parents to three beautiful children, ponder the thought of who this package could have come from, an emotional shockwave seems to impact Queen.

"Jared, what if it is from –" is all he could hear her utter before a gust of wind carried her voice away from his listening ears.

Queen slowly lifts the book out of the box as if she is holding a delicate glass that she doesn't want to chip or break. Her buttery soft palm begins to trace over the book's cover as she fixates her gaze on the front.

opens book

Understand

Stop... Feel the book in your hands... its texture... its thickness... its lightweight. It's definitely lighter than the air currently surrounding you.

Wait, maybe not. Extend your arm forward and hold it there... straight forward... absolutely perpendicular to your body with your palm facing upwards. Hold the air... the air that is so weightless... the air that you walk through easily... the air that you inhale... exhale... so easily day in and day out.

Don't put your hand down. I need you to continue to hold the air that is deemed weightless by mankind.

Now understand that this story is about someone you love, care for, and cherish with all of your heart, mind, body, and soul. Somebody that you would sacrifice your own life for if it meant saving theirs. Imagine

their face... water slowly covering their eyes, creating a glistening appearance... the water slowly collecting as if it is about to overflow... until the pool reaches its maximum capacity. Each tear begins falling... slowly... ever so gently down their cheek... rolling down their face to be dropped and never seen again.

A burden just like the air. Weightless, while weight filled.

Tears filled with feelings. Full of emotion, too much to hold.

Feel his burden of adaptability.

Start

Queen sits up & begins reading...

-

Once Mrs. Cane... Now Mrs. Ocean... Always my mother...

Well, hey, mom... I know that it has been about eight years since we last saw each other face to face. It hurts me a lot, so I know it has to hurt you too. So now, please listen to me just this once, and let me try and describe my emotions to you.

If you could imagine the sharpest blade that you know. Do you remember the ones that you wouldn't let Kara, Prince, & I use to cook with since they were those costly kitchen knives? The ones that you got when we were kids... remember? Well, maybe you do, perhaps you don't, maybe it's just me... however, I remember how you could slice through all of the meat and vegetables so easily. Then, you would cook them for our family to eat, give us life, and provide each of our bodies nourishment. Well, honestly, I feel like that was me... like the food was me. It felt as if my heart was sliced open by those oh-so-special knives of yours... to uncontrollably pour out love, kindness, and joy for my own blood… all just to be taken in by everyone else, ultimately forgotten shortly thereafter. Just like now… I am forgotten.

-

Her eyes begin to accompany her sweat glands… leaking water time after time.

-

And I don't say any of those words for sympathy; I say them to only convey my feelings and emotions of how I felt… how I think. A pointless effort to tell and explain to you what I was never given a chance to do before. And of course, you and dad are great parents, so don't question that even though you probably are by now. You guys raised me in a loving environment with two supportive siblings, all in a completely stable household. For that, I appreciate you both immensely.

I wrote you this in part to say thank you. Thank you for helping me get to where I am today and aiding me in achieving all that I have achieved today. I wouldn't have been able to create an architectural empire, become the most prominent fighter against climate change, or develop the world's largest and most successful law firm fighting racial injustices. I wouldn't have been able to change the world in such impactful ways for my people, my community, my family & friends… well… I'm just saying that I wouldn't have been able to change the world if it wasn't for you all. So, I genuinely thank you for that.

-

Queen looks up at Jared with tear-filled eyes… streams of tears and sweat flowing in unison down her plump cheeks.

-

I remember when you told me that I had to be able to pivot throughout life… that I couldn't solely focus on planning, and that I had to go for things along with the flow of life. "To be able to adapt" is how you had once put it. To be able to change with the times. To be able to adjust to any situation no matter what life throws at you and find a way. To be adaptable.

You told me that I was different and could take on the world if I learned, and look at me now… I did it, mom. I really did change the world just as you said that I could, but now when I look back… when I look back at the divide between us… I want to change it because now I am all alone.

Yet, despite this, I'm appreciative of my experiences. I learned how life works and operates… how it will throw absolutely anything and everything, at you to try and knock you off balance. However, at the end of the day, you must catch yourself or try to at least break the fall. And most importantly, the crucial fact of life that no one could ever fight against it for me… except for me. And despite my pain and strife, the lack of a complete family, I learned that much, at least.

Maybe… possibly… well… what it feels like to me is that I did it perhaps a bit too well with everything… with everybody. Because everyone is in your life for a season, right? It can be for a specific reason… it can be for a season… even in rare cases, for a lifetime. That's what everyone says, at least. But, do you know what everyone says as well? They say that they won't or that someone can't fade away… but they never seem to be able to leave out the fact that anything in life could happen. Sometimes, it feels as if they knew this was exactly how it would end up. That at the end of the day, I would be here… alone… while they are happy with new and better people.

At the same time, I kind of feel when these things are coming, which is why I was able to... ya know... adapt... use that thing that I became proficient in. Maybe that's why people leave me and walk out of my life at that slow and steady pace as if they don't want me to notice, even though I can see it all happening in even slower motion. Maybe, just maybe, it's because they know that I will be fine... that I will be okay... but I just want to be good enough... to not have to adapt to everything, even things that I don't desire.

-

Queen slowly rolled from flat on her stomach and onto her right side.

"Hey, honey, do you think that we were good parents," Queen managed to say as her broken voice attempted to fight against her emotion-filled tears.

Jared's gaze shifted from the absolutely pristine, clear blue water of the expansive ocean out in front of them and onto his seemingly heartbroken wife.

"Queen, what happened? What did you read," he questions as he slowly sits up from the comfort of his dark blue beach chair. He then begins to move

towards his wife with his arms outstretched as if shielding her from the world's pain.

-

And sometimes I wish I didn't have to be here all alone... well, all of the time, if I am sincere.

Wait a second. I just remembered that I need to tell you about where I am. Well, over the past number of years, I have been constructing this enormous self-sustaining island. The weather here is always beautiful, just as I always liked it. Not too hot, but just the perfect temperature that you feel warm inside and out, but not sweating to the point that you get uncomfortable. Genuinely, it's like a paradise. I'm looking up at the sky from my dark blue lawn chair that I used to use at your grandkids' soccer games. I hope they visit you more than they do me... but I guess that wouldn't be too hard... they never tried to come around after leaving.

Every now and then, I can look up and see these light-brown hawks with a white stripe around its neck, almost like a little dog collar, swiftly flying through the sky. They always have this meticulous look on their faces and a weird-feeling aura about them that makes it feel like they are getting ready to hunt. I've seen them swoop down so fast and eat a couple of these dark gray, 3-foot snakes, some little brown mice, and even a few tiny little blue birds here and there too.

The ocean is absolutely pristine, with water so clear that I can see the sand below the water even sitting from here 10 yards away from the shore. Just like the private beach I bought for you and dad many years ago... it reminds me of you guys out here. I wish you all were here... maybe this was how it was supposed to be though.

Anyway, that is where I am. No, I can't tell you where I am even though you are my mom; that was the entire point of this all. I'll adapt to this life just like every other time. Like any other time, even though I never wanted to be alone... be the one left wanting, begging for more... and what is different now than before? Right, nothing.

-

The beautiful, sun-filled sky morphed into a gloomy, dark grey cloud-filled sky within the brief time since the book was opened.

Queen slowly rolled from laying on her right side and onto her back before sitting straight up on her towel. As she tries to lift her head to look up at Jared, her

chin drops back down as if it was forcefully pushed down by someone behind her. Coincidingly, her heart cries tears that could cause the ocean before her to overflow... with her eyes shutting as her head falls.

She opens her eyes, peering through the fog created by her tears, and looks at the same book you're reading right now as she holds it in her right hand. A perfect-sized book... not too big... not too small. Not extremely daunting nor underwhelming. Gazing at the cover of this book, she reads,

But guess what…

I love me
I love who I am
I love who I was born to be
I love who I was destined to be
I love who I am zestfully

This is My Burden Of Adaptability

His
Burden Of
Blissfulness

Jared Ocean

To be the burden

To know a burden
To know how heavy a load things can be
To know how they can affect a person
To know how to deal with a burden

To see a burden
To see what damage it can inflict
To see what unbearable weight drags behind
To see what immense dream can be crushed

To be a burden
To be the creator of turmoil in a life
To be the reason a family has a strife
To be the reason another life has no light

To be the burden
To know a burden
To see a burden
To be a burden
And above all else
Try your hardest not
To be THE burden
The burden to all but you
Yet you are THE burden
The burden to none but you

Opening

opens box

Standing tall with a broad stance, almost like a sturdy mahogany tree that can't be pushed over or broken down, Mr. Ocean holds the box slightly in front of him.

Looking down into his freshly opened cardboard box, he sees a book. A perfect-sized book... not too big... not too small. Not extremely daunting nor underwhelming. He sees the exact book you're reading right now lying perfectly inside the small cardboard box he just opened up. Gazing at the cover of this book, he reads, "His Burden Of Blissfulness."

Mr. Ocean slowly turns away from the light brown beach house door as he continues to have his gaze fixated on the cover of this book... *His Burden of Blissfulness.*

"Bliss...," he says to himself ever so quietly, as if whispering it to himself.

"Joy... happiness... infinite joy and happiness," Mr. Ocean repeats to himself three times.

A look of recollection... remembrance... maybe a look of nostalgia comes across his face, but his face doesn't tell the whole story of what he truly feels. Perhaps it's the look of a person who just remembered a deeply traumatizing experience... no one... not even his wife, would ever be able to decipher the look on his face at this very moment.

"To find bliss... to be blissfully ignorant... to protect and provide my family with a beautiful life. Enhance their lives and mental condition to a state of bliss... that's really all I ever tried to do...," whispers Mr. Ocean as a tear slowly slid down his face.

Mr. Ocean knows who this book has come from before reading a single page... simply off of reading the title.

"You will find happiness in pursuing your dreams, my son. Find joy in changing the lives of all the people you have touched. And most importantly, find bliss at the end of it all. Just be sure to be selfless no matter what," he says aloud before pausing.

Slowly raising his head, he looks into the expansive room that he finds himself in at this very moment.

His head slowly turns to the left and begins scanning the room… taking in every little detail; from the dark hallway in the back-left corner of the room that leads to the master bedroom and shower, to the back wall, which is completely made of reinforced glass window panes exposing the current dark clouded… rain filled-sky.

As he takes a seat in his dark-brown, leather rocking chair, his scan of the room completes. His gaze then fixates upon the beautiful and elegantly painted family portrait from years ago… and he remembers the memorable vacation he took with his family.

His eyes slowly sink deeper into a realm of sadness as he is reminded of the reality of the so-called "family portrait" that contains four bright smiles.

opens book

Understand

Stop... Feel the book in your hands... its texture... its thickness... its lightweight. It's definitely lighter than the air currently surrounding you.

Wait, maybe not. Extend your arm forward and hold it there... straight forward... absolutely perpendicular to your body with your palm facing upwards. Hold the air... the air that is so weightless... the air that you walk through easily... the air that you inhale... exhale... so easily day in and day out.

Don't put your hand down. I need you to continue to hold the air that is deemed weightless by mankind.

Now understand that this story is about someone you love, care for, and cherish with all of your heart, mind, body, and soul. Somebody that you would sacrifice your own life for if it meant saving theirs. Imagine

their face... water slowly covering their eye, creating a glistening appearance... the water slowly collecting as if it is about to overflow... until the pool reaches its maximum capacity. Each tear begins falling... slowly... ever so gently down their cheek... rolling down their face to be dropped and never seen again.

A burden just like the air. Weightless, while weight filled.

Tears filled with feelings. Full of emotion, too much to hold.

Feel his burden of Blissfulness.

Start

Mr. Ocean looks back down and begins reading…

-

Hey Mr. Ocean… Jared Ocean…

I just wanted to thank you for everything you did for me… mom… my little sister & my brother…

You taught me how to be not only a man, but also a gentleman in this wild, wild world that we live in today. Looking back on it, it's such an enormous blessing to have grown up in this two-parent household with a father that loves my mother. I've seen so many of my friends, people that I care for, and even strangers treated poorly by their parents… the people that made them… the people that were supposed to care for them. So, I truly appreciate you for being a great father, Dad.

And I know that mom got her package first… I purposefully set it up that way. So, please continue to do what you do, shield her from her negative emotions, and ensure that she's all good. I have a gut feeling that you have been, or at least been trying to since she read hers since you guys are always joined at the hip.

-

Just as he hears the sound of the shower water in the back left side of the beach house fade away, his first tear is accompanied by another... following the exact path of the first.

-

One of my dreams was to always be like you, Dad... I've always wanted to have a wife... kids... a true family of my own. However, I couldn't ever seem to grasp how you did it... not even with Zhuri... and since then, I guess I never really tried. I even had to adopt kids since I seemingly couldn't have ones of my own. However, I think it helps out the world, and I really do believe that I saved some children's lives. Still, nonetheless, they don't even seem to like... appreciate... even love me... so, maybe it really is just me. I am the common denominator through this all.

With every woman I have ever been interested in... with every woman I have ever loved... it's almost as if my well of love never ran out. Why is that? I always wanted to ask you why you thought that that was... what you believed I did wrong... because you could capture true love with mom. You created a world of truthfully ignorant bliss for Prince, Kara, & me throughout our childhoods in order to protect us from the tragedies and violence of the world, and we all love you for that. At least I know that I do.

I was always… I still am always. Well, maybe I'm delusional, but I am still always full of happiness… joy… blissfulness… all because of how you taught me to live, love, and grow.

-

Mr. Ocean feels a slightly cold yet comforting, damp hand come to rest upon his right cheek… gently wiping his pair of tears away.

"We are amazing parents," Queen says. "Just as you told me when we were just outside, Yes, we did our best job."

-

I've always been in a state of bliss, so it made it extremely easy to steadily live how you told me to. It made minor conflicts and inconveniences seem so minute that I never wallowed over the smaller things. I never let the little things throughout life ruin or negatively impact a relationship or friendship, whether it be with family, a lover, or a friend. By doing this, I was able to negate unnecessary conflict and feel ready to create the change that I wanted to see in the world no matter how much hate was thrown at me. I thank you for that… to the moon and back, Dad.

However, even despite my efforts to maintain this mindset, it didn't seem enough to keep anybody around. So, I had to escape the world and am currently alone on an island. The weather here is absolutely perfect here; "hooping weather," as you would say. Speaking of, I have a regulation-size indoor basketball court with freshly waxed hardwood. It's absolutely insane, and I wish you could see it because it looks exactly like how I told you I dreamed it would so many years ago. I just hoped that we could've played here together, but the court remains untouched… no blemishes… free of the memory of a single game.

I wanted to be like you… have a family like yours, so I bought myself a dark blue mesh lawn chair. I used to use it at my children's soccer games. It's funny because it's the same brand of chair that you had when Kara and Prince broke it that one time… the dark blue one that had the bent leg. I miss those days.

There are also these birds, I forgot what they're called, but they look like seagulls, yet they're jet black. Their feathers flutter through the sky slightly as they soar through the sky, cruising at a relaxed pace. The ocean is absolutely pristine, with water so clear that I can see the sand below the water even sitting from here 10 yards away from the shore. You would love it here... well, anyone would really... but I'm the only one.

And just like you told me every time something seemed to be going on, "You were good," and "would be okay." So, there's no need to worry about me. Just make sure that you are good. Take care of mom, Kara, and Prince, and just let them know that I will be... well, that I am good.

My state of bliss could have possibly blinded me from some truths and realities of this world that we live in... the "cold, cold world," as some would say. Yet, I don't see it as that for some reason. The more I think about it, maybe that reason is because you taught me that I was capable of changing the world. So, I want to say thank you for everything... maybe even blame you for everything.

-

"I'm so sorry," he repeats over… and over… and over again as if he hoped it would somehow reach the ears that he so wanted the apology to land upon.

The sound waves take a trip around the room… bouncing off of the walls… the table… every object in the entire room; continually echoing over and over without ever finding ears to land on. With each repetition… the sounds get quieter and quieter… until the room becomes hushed again.

-

To find bliss… to be blissfully ignorant… to protect and provide my family with a beautiful life… enhance their lives and mental condition to a stable state. That's really all I ever really tried to do, all that I ever really wanted to do.

"I will find happiness in pursuing my dreams. I will find joy in changing the lives of all the people I have touched. I will find bliss at the end of it all, as long as I am selfless no matter what."

That is one of the many daily affirmations you taught me, and I remember it to this day. So, I will continue to think to myself, maybe this is what bliss truly is. It may be a place only I can go, no matter how much I want anyone else to go. I don't know if it is, but I still trust you, so I will continue to live like this because everyone else seems happy. And that is all that matters... So, I will remain here in a state of "bliss."

-

Mr. Ocean leans back into his leather chair, that is still cold to the touch. The chair envelops him as he sinks into the crease. He leans the chair as far as he can as if trying to lay the emotions to rest, but he feels them becoming too much to hold. Raising his right hand from the side of the chair, he holds the book with a grip that could never be pried away. Then, his eyelids slowly shut...

Mr. Ocean opens his eyes, peering through the fog created by his tears, and looks at the exact book you're reading right now as he holds it in his right hand. A perfect-sized book... not too big... not too small. Not extremely daunting nor underwhelming. Gazing at the cover of this book, he reads,

But guess what…

I love me
I love who I am
I love who I was born to be
I love who I was destined to be
I love who I am adaptively

This is My Burden Of Blissfulness

His
Burden Of
Carefulness

Leroy Henderson

To be the burden

To know a burden

To know how heavy a load things can be
To know how they can affect a person
To know how to deal with a burden

To see a burden

To see what damage it can inflict
To see what unbearable weight drags behind
To see what immense dream can be crushed

To be a burden

To be the creator of turmoil in a life
To be the reason a family has a strife
To be the reason another life has no light

To be the burden

To know a burden
To see a burden
To be a burden
And above all else
Try your hardest not
To be THE burden
The burden to all but you
Yet you are THE burden
The burden to none but you

Understand

Stop... Feel the book in your hands... its texture... its thickness... its lightweight. It's definitely lighter than the air currently surrounding you.

Wait, maybe not. Extend your arm forward and hold it there... straight forward... absolutely perpendicular to your body with your palm facing upwards. Hold the air... the air that is so weightless... the air that you walk through easily... the air that you inhale... exhale... so easily day in and day out.

Don't put your hand down. I need you to continue to hold the air that is deemed weightless by mankind.

Now understand that this story is about someone you love, care for, and cherish with all of your heart, mind, body, and soul. Somebody that you would sacrifice your own life for if it meant saving theirs. Imagine

their face... water slowly covering their eye, creating a glistening appearance... the water slowly collecting as if it is about to overflow... until the pool reaches its maximum capacity and each tear begins falling... slowly... ever so gently down their cheek... rolling down their face to be dropped and never seen again.

A burden just like the air. Weightless, while weight filled.

Tears filled with feelings. Full of emotion, too much to hold.

Feel his burden of Carefulness.

<u>Stairs</u>

Can't trust all of these empty stares
Consistently up to something

Sly eyes greeting their mirror –
 accompanied by a bright smile –
  the twist of a cold, hard knob –
This, a purely fine-tuned process
A process, taken step by step

One – Mindlessly, giving a smile back
Two – Foolishly, greeting those sly eyes right back
Three – My body slowly descends,
 Following the guidance of these stares
  One by one…
   Step-by-step…

But guess what…

I love me
I love who I am
I love who I was born to be
I love who I was destined to be
I love who I am blissfully

This is My Burden Of Carefulness

His Burden Of Dedication

Lane Robinson

To be the burden

To know a burden
To know how heavy a load things can be
To know how they can affect a person
To know how to deal with a burden

To see a burden
To see what damage it can inflict
To see what unbearable weight drags behind
To see what immense dream can be crushed

To be a burden
To be the creator of turmoil in a life
To be the reason a family has a strife
To be the reason another life has no light

To be the burden
To know a burden
To see a burden
To be a burden
And above all else
Try your hardest not
To be THE burden
The burden to all but you
Yet you are THE burden
The burden to none but you

Understand

Stop... Feel the book in your hands... its texture... its thickness... its lightweight. It's definitely lighter than the air currently surrounding you.

Wait, maybe not. Extend your arm forward and hold it there... straight forward... absolutely perpendicular to your body with your palm facing upwards. Hold the air... the air that is so weightless... the air that you walk through easily... the air that you inhale... exhale... so easily day in and day out.

Don't put your hand down. I need you to continue to hold the air that is deemed weightless by mankind.

Now understand that this story is about someone you love, care for, and cherish with all of your heart, mind, body, and soul. Somebody that you would sacrifice your own life for if it meant saving theirs. Imagine

their face... water slowly covering their eye, creating a glistening appearance... the water slowly collecting as if it is about to overflow... until the pool reaches its maximum capacity. Each tear begins falling... slowly... ever so gently down their cheek... rolling down their face to be dropped and never seen again.

A burden just like the air. Weightless, while weight filled.

Tears filled with feelings. Full of emotion, too much to hold.

Feel his burden of Dedication.

The Estuary Of Dreams

Part 1 - The Stream

Like a vast school of fish

My dreams pool together

Shining as bright as the Sun

The perfect habitat for hopes and thoughts

Mimicking the yellow of the Sun

Part 2 - The River

Their enemy?

My doubts

Skillfully camouflaged, scales holding blue

Pain, strife, and trauma of the past

Deep down below, they grew

Part 3 - The Mouth

So innocent…

So sweet…

My beautiful Suns sparkle in the pond

Unaware of their natural blue counterparts

Existing not too far beyond

Part 4 - The Estuary

The blue dragging yellow down where no one could go

Consuming one another in ways no one could know

Lifeless bodies and blood filling the water –

    or so it seems…

But sometimes, you may see a sparkle of green

Oh, what a wonderful show in the estuary of dreams

But guess what…

I love me
I love who I am
I love who I was born to be
I love who I was destined to be
I love who I am carefully

This is My Burden Of Dedication

His
Burden Of
Exceptionality

Zhuri Prime

To be the burden

To know a burden
To know how heavy a load things can be
To know how they can affect a person
To know how to deal with a burden

To see a burden
To see what damage it can inflict
To see what unbearable weight drags behind
To see what immense dream can be crushed

To be a burden
To be the creator of turmoil in a life
To be the reason a family has a strife
To be the reason another life has no light

To be the burden
To know a burden
To see a burden
To be a burden
And above all else
Try your hardest not
To be THE burden
The burden to all but you
Yet you are THE burden
The burden to none but you

Opening

opens box

A gentle breeze brushes up against her soft, smooth, melanin-filled skin.

The mahogany doorframe holds sturdy as she gazes out into the expansive acreage filled with greenery outside the Prime mansion. The full moon illuminates the deep, dark blues of the hydrangeas, while simultaneously expressing the bright reds and pinks of the bountiful rose bushes leading up the driveway.

Looking down into her freshly opened cardboard box, she sees a book. A perfect-sized book... not too big... not too small. Not extremely daunting nor underwhelming. She sees the exact book you're reading right now, lying perfectly inside the small cardboard box she just opened. Gazing at the cover of this book reads, "His Burden Of Exceptionality."

She slowly transitions her gaze from upon the book, ever so gently, with her eyes moving before her head towards the star-flooded sky. Her dark brown eyes fill with spectacle as she surveys the stars... while her tears join together in community at the bottom corners of her eyes as her soul builds up with emotion and wonder.

Her eyelids shut so slowly and gently as if they are trying not to create a splash that would initiate a waterfall in the community of tears in her eyes.

As she takes a deep breath...

inhales

exhales

... a star in which she can not see with her blinded eyes streaks brightly across the starry night.

As she gathers her composure, she steps back inside her mansion. Somehow through the emotion-filled night, she garners the strength to shut the heavy, custom-carved mahogany door. As she pushes the door closed, she feels the deep carvings, intricate designs, and meaningful images held by this masterpiece.

This beautiful, dark brown mahogany wood door was installed when she had the house built many years ago by a past mention.

She turns around and walks through her house. With each step, you can hear a slight echo due to her house's sheer amount of space. She walks through the hallway that is filled with art from the past two centuries that she thoroughly loves. Slowly making her way to her bedroom, she picks up her ZP plush throw that she always takes with her to bed.

Slowly but steadily, she gets to her bedroom, where she immediately throws the book onto her bed, causing it to spin like a frisbee.

ding

"You received a text message from Claire. Would you like me to read it to you, Zhuri," reads the speaker in Zhuri's room.

"No, thank you," she replies as she changes and joins her book in her double king-sized bed filled with blankets and pillows. "I guess I should read this now, shouldn't I," she says as she questions herself aloud.

"Yes, you should," replies her speaker.

opens book

Understand

Stop… Feel the book in your hands… its texture… its thickness… its lightweight. It's definitely lighter than the air currently surrounding you.

Wait, maybe not. Extend your arm forward and hold it there… straight forward… absolutely perpendicular to your body with your palm facing upwards. Hold the air… the air that is so weightless… the air that you walk through easily… the air that you inhale… exhale… so easily day in and day out.

Don't put your hand down. I need you to continue to hold the air that is deemed weightless by mankind.

Now understand that this story is about someone you love, care for, and cherish with all of your heart, mind, body, and soul. Somebody that you would sacrifice your own life for if it meant saving theirs. Imagine

their face… water slowly covering their eye, creating a glistening appearance… the water slowly collecting as if it is about to overflow… until the pool reaches its maximum capacity. Each tear begins falling… slowly… ever so gently down their cheek… rolling down their face to be dropped and never seen again.

A burden just like the air. Weightless, while weight filled.

Tears filled with feelings. Full of emotion, too much to hold.

Feel his burden of Exceptionality.

Start

Zhuri sits up & begins reading...

-

Zhuri Prime, the person that had my heart in their grasp tighter than anyone else in this world. The person I truly entrusted my heart with and cared about more than anyone throughout this journey we call life. The one that showed me that it was perfectly fine to be different. That it was a blessing to be exceptionally exceptional.

I remember that bright light that you described to me. You know... the light that seems to shine ultimately enveloping the Earth... this light that attempts to surpass the grandiose chain reaction of nuclear fission that the Sun unleashes... Me.

Being the light to the world isn't something that just anybody can do because everyone isn't strong enough, moreso willing enough, to do so. Unbeknownst to you though, this exceptionality is what created this finely ground, warm sand under my freshly pedicured, brown feet.

-

Zhuri removes the plush blanket wrapped around her like a baby and slides her feet off the bed to the right one by one. She looks down and begins reading the writing again.

-

It's apparent that I'm not the norm. A genius… an enigma… an anomaly, some may say. I am an exception. And I understand being different. I understand being exceptional. But to be exceptional with exception to my deepest desires… why must that be me.

-

Zhuri begins to walk through her bedroom as if she is entirely out of touch with reality… no conscious thought… no sense of direction… but absolutely knows where she is going.

She saunters… one foot after another… taking a single step every two seconds without creating a single squeak due to her house's perfect foundation and construction.

-

Well, I am on an island right now. Over the past... well, lots of years, I have been constructing this self-sustaining island. The weather here is always in the 80s... never ever cold... sun steady beaming... birds singing elegant songs... a slight breeze that cools you off to the perfect temperature. I'm looking up at the sky from my lawn chair. You would absolutely love it here, Z... well, anyone would really... but unfortunately, I'm the only one.

I don't want to be the only one, though. So, how come I have to be the only one... why can I build an empire spanning the world that has the influence of an entire country, but I can't be genuinely loved?

-

Zhuri's eyes begin to quiver, blurring her vision even more than before as she makes her way down the stairs.

-

Right here on this island is just like where everyone would have put me if they could have... alone... all alone... on an island to do everything that I could ever want. I'm able to have every materialistic desire from a basketball court with freshly polished hardwood, to an ATV course that winds through the deep deciduous forest, to my own bowling alley. All my own... all that I wanted... all that anyone could ever want... but to enjoy it alone... to not be worth the time of day to anybody... to have it all and left alone. How come it's always like that for me? Why am I always the one wanting more?

I mean... I never found a wife through my numerous attempts at relationships, sadly enough. Not that I thought it would be any different, honestly, because of how different I am... because of how different I function... because my heart isn't large enough.

I adopted four children some years back... a 15-year-old Ghanaian girl, a 13-year-old Senegalese boy, and a set of 10-year-old twin girls from the Ivory Coast. They're gone now, and they never came back, so I don't believe I did enough. I really wasn't ever enough to anybody, even my own kids after I saved them from tragic situations in each their own respect. If I truly did do enough, then it would be different. Maybe I wouldn't be all alone on this island right now. But really, all I want is to be free, so I had to do this.

I created a foundation in which no one that I care about and cherish so deeply has to ever worry about their next meal... if they would sleep safely each night... whether they will be able to pursue their dreams. Please tell me why I can do that, but no one else seems to be able to like me... why me. Why can I have everything... create everything... everything except for genuine love.

A perfect example is with you, Zhuri. Four joy-filled, laughter-fueled years passed before I built you the Prime Mansion. I believed that that was true love. It felt like true love to me, even though it must have been a thorough and drawn-out facade. I thought I could have somewhat controlled a bit of that. Nonetheless, I guess you have memories of me, right? Maybe you remember the custom mahogany door that I had hand-crafted for you... holding the memories of each of our ancestors and our people's actual, rich history. Perhaps you've realized the subtlety of never hearing a pesky squeak on the dark, hard, wooden floor. Perhaps you adore the art elegantly enveloping the hallways in size and color order just as you like. At least I hope because I always tried my hardest to love.

And you know, I've always wondered if you ever moved in there or if you still believe it is wrong to receive from a heart that you broke. One day... maybe one day, you will forgive yourself because I never have had or will have ill will towards you. Just like with you, I always only had one goal: to create a world in which everyone's life that I touch is even happier during and after my involvement in theirs. I wish someone cared to do that for me too.

-

Zhuri looks to her left... and to her right... as the colorful acrylic paintings, elegantly signed *Scarlet Love*, begin to melt right before her eyes. The various vibrant colors of bright red and banana yellow mixing with the cool and rich colors of swampy green and royal blue. Watching the art grow smaller... and smaller... she continues to progress down the quiet, dark hallway towards the front door.

Zhuri reaches her front door once again... holding a perfect-sized book... not too big... not too small. Not extremely daunting nor underwhelming.

She opens up the sturdy mahogany door and steps outside of the sturdy mahogany doorframe. A gentle breeze brushes up against her soft, smooth, melanin-filled skin. Her gaze extends out and across the expansive acreage filled with greenery outside of the Prime mansion. She looks upon the full moon, which still illuminates the night sky... giving light to the deep, dark blues of the hydrangeas... showing off the bright reds and pinks of the bountiful rose bushes leading up the driveway.

Zhuri's balance begins to wane as she feels her body lean slightly forward... backward... to the right... and to the left... with the dizziness starting to become overwhelming. Finally, she takes a seat on the cool marble that envelops her porch with her feet on the stair right below where she is sitting.

Her head drops between her knees as if it was forcefully pushed down by someone behind her as she cries tears that could cause the oceans to overflow. Zhuri cries a cry so loud that maybe even he could hear it.

She opens her eyes, peering through the fog created by her tears, and looks at the exact book you're reading right now as she holds it in her right hand. A perfect-sized book... not too big... not too small. Not extremely daunting nor underwhelming. Gazing at the cover of this book, she reads,

But guess what...

I love me
I love who I am
I love who I was born to be
I love who I was destined to be
I love who I am fearlessly

This is My Burden Of Exceptionality

His
Burden Of
Fearlessness

Kofi Ocean

To be the burden

To know a burden
To know how heavy a load things can be
To know how they can affect a person
To know how to deal with a burden

To see a burden
To see what damage it can inflict
To see what unbearable weight drags behind
To see what immense dream can be crushed

To be a burden
To be the creator of turmoil in a life
To be the reason a family has a strife
To be the reason another life has no light

To be the burden
To know a burden
To see a burden
To be a burden
And above all else
Try your hardest not
To be THE burden
The burden to all but you
Yet you are THE burden
The burden to none but you

Understand

Stop... Feel the book in your hands... its texture... its thickness... its lightweight. It's definitely lighter than the air currently surrounding you.

Wait, maybe not. Extend your arm forward and hold it there... straight forward... absolutely perpendicular to your body with your palm facing upwards. Hold the air... the air that is so weightless... the air that you walk through easily... the air that you inhale... exhale... so easily day in and day out.

Don't put your hand down. I need you to continue to hold the air that is deemed weightless by mankind.

Now understand that this story is about someone you love, care for, and cherish with all of your heart, mind, body, and soul. Somebody that you would sacrifice your own life for if it meant saving theirs. Imagine

their face... water slowly covering their eye, creating a glistening appearance... the water slowly collecting as if it is about to overflow... until the pool reaches its maximum capacity. Each tear begins falling... slowly... ever so gently down their cheek... rolling down their face to be dropped and never seen again.

A burden just like the air. Weightless, while weight filled.

Tears filled with feelings. Full of emotion, too much to hold.

Feel his burden of Fearlessness.

<u>Beyond Skin</u>

Our rich history as brown as a tree
The mother atop the hierarchy
Meaning the Royal blood flows through the Queens
Yet this ancestral history's hidden from you and me

"Don't be like your father!
Be harder – Think smarter –
Destined to fail and end up in jail
Cause like him,
    You're quite a few shades darker."

My hero subject to constant erasure
Books vandalized, ripped up paper
"Let me learn," I beg,
With my freshly cut taper

It's deeper than simply my black skin
Her hair's porosity can hold the water of the sea –

While theirs is curled…
    resemblant of tightly curled springs
Concurrent with mine loc'd with history…
    and his is wavy like the sea

Yet, from sea to sea, my people have been spread
Forced upon us a different place to lay our head
Slave trade… gentrification… and injustice
But always looking out and sure to break bread

We always appreciate our chances
Enjoying ourselves and sharing dances
That somehow want to get stolen
Despite the constant demeaning glances

So, I won't ever have a prison in my picture…
And don't ever try and break up my family picture…
My spirit forever knows what's held beyond my skin…
So, don't you dare try and taint what I know is within

But guess what…

I love me
I love who I am
I love who I was born to be
I love who I was destined to be
I love who I am exceptionally

This is My Burden Of Fearlessness

His
Burden Of
Gratitude

Danielle Blue

To be the burden

To know a burden
To know how heavy a load things can be
To know how they can affect a person
To know how to deal with a burden

To see a burden
To see what damage it can inflict
To see what unbearable weight drags behind
To see what immense dream can be crushed

To be a burden
To be the creator of turmoil in a life
To be the reason a family has a strife
To be the reason another life has no light

To be the burden
To know a burden
To see a burden
To be a burden
And above all else
Try your hardest not
To be THE burden
The burden to all but you
Yet you are THE burden
The burden to none but you

Opening

opens box

A strong, young, black mother... fully protective over her child with her maternal instincts... succumbing to no pressures or downfalls.

"Never let them see you without a smile on your face Danielle. Not everyone is genuine, and they may take advantage of your weakness. Promise me, Danielle... that you will never let them see your vulnerability."

That was what the mother of Mrs. Danielle Blue told her when she was growing up. So, she won't ever allow anyone to ever see a frown or tear on her face. Just some years back though, Danielle was a charming and beautiful Jamaican mother, who became pregnant as she journeyed through higher education.

She battled with her job, being a first-generation student, a broken family, and raising a black child in white America as an immigrant, among a multitude of other hardships that she had to face. However, she always remembered the promise that her mother made her make when she was a child.

Mrs. Blue knew firsthand how hard mental health could genuinely affect a person's soul, especially at the various young, pivotal ages in life. So, she created *Our Promise*.

Our Promise is a children's mental health non-profit business that aims to provide children and families with the opportunities, skills, and tools to help fight mental health battles. Prior to its inception, there was nothing out there like it. Communities and people worldwide believed depression and anxiety to be a myth... a label of a detrimental illness that could never be cured.

Plus, each and every year due to a mammoth-sized donation made by an unknown philanthropist, numerous programs, initiatives, and events have been able to be funded. For example, today is the event of the year for the community, a firework show.

She usually is extremely excited as this spectacular event comes closer to its commencement each year. She would envision how the night would go while sitting in her dressing room, ecstatic for what's next, and imagine how the night sky would look as it is filled with colorful lights.

However, this year the energy in the setting felt unusual, abnormal from the previous years' energies.

Currently, in the dressing room sits Mrs. Blue before her 50-inch x 50-inch mirror with a white LED-lit frame.

Sitting in the reflection is a mask of a smile... bolded mascara and elaborate eyeshadow... makeup around the cheeks... shadows to enunciate facial structure. A mask aiming to draw attention away from its partner's discolored eyes... stress-induced pimples... withering eyelids, and eye bags.

And below the mask sits a face holding back tears... pain... anxiety... agony... weakness. But how could she show the person behind the mask? That is not who she is... who she is seen to be throughout this world.

So, she steadily sits with her emotions flowing through her heart... a face full of make-up... a mind full of thoughts...

A few moments later, she hears a booming voice coming from the long hallway outside the dressing room.

"Where is Mrs. Blue," yells a voice so stern that it casts a shockwave throughout all that its sound falls upon.

In mere moments, everyone's eyes will be taped to the sky as the most spectacular show in the tri-state area commences.

As footsteps shuffle across the wooden floors of the lakeside clubhouse, another voice responds, "It's almost time! We can't have any delays, or the show will not be perfect!"

"Where is Mrs. Blue? It is almost time," speaks a faint voice, buffered by the insulated dressing room door.

Looking down into her freshly opened cardboard box, she sees a book. A perfect-sized book... not too big... not too small. Not extremely daunting nor underwhelming. She sees the exact book you're reading right now, lying perfectly inside the small cardboard box she just opened. Gazing at the cover of this book, she reads, "His Burden Of Gratitude."

"But it was our promise," says Mrs. Blue silently to herself.

opens book

Understand

Stop... Feel the book in your hands... its texture... its thickness... its lightweight. It's definitely lighter than the air currently surrounding you.

Wait, maybe not. Extend your arm forward and hold it there... straight forward... absolutely perpendicular to your body with your palm facing upwards. Hold the air... the air that is so weightless... the air that you walk through easily... the air that you inhale... exhale... so easily day in and day out.

Don't put your hand down. I need you to continue to hold the air that is deemed weightless by mankind.

Now understand that this story is about someone you love, care for, and cherish with all of your heart, mind, body, and soul. Somebody that you would sacrifice your own life for if it meant saving theirs. Imagine

their face... water slowly covering their eye, creating a glistening appearance... the water slowly collecting as if it is about to overflow... until the pool reaches its maximum capacity and each tear begins falling... slowly... ever so gently down their cheek... rolling down their face to be dropped and never seen again.

A burden just like the air. Weightless, while weight filled.

Tears filled with feelings. Full of emotion, too much to hold.

Feel his burden of Gratitude.

Danielle begins reading...

-

My life feels like, in a way, that I was given a 10-piece puzzle...

That I was given this mystery to solve while everyone else was handed a 1,000-piece puzzle... handed a 1,000-piece puzzle, told to leave the comfort of their mother's womb, and tasked with figuring out this thing we call "life."

It just doesn't seem fair. It doesn't seem fair to me at all. Why is it that this experience we call life only took a few pieces to join together before it all made sense to me? How come everyone I talk to doesn't seem to understand what I'm able to see?

Maybe it is really just that the few pieces I have just make up a more significant piece of my puzzle. I don't know.

Sometimes I just wish that someone else understood life as me, despite its various intricacies. But, honestly, I thought that you did for a while.

-

"Mrs. Blue, where are you," yells another voice from down the long, narrow hallway, seemingly coming closer to the dressing room. However, as her mask begins to melt, Danielle continues to read.

-

When you first told me about *Our Promise*, I absolutely loved the idea, and I still do. That is why I pledged $50 million over the first 20 years after its inception.

Your vision to create a children's mental health non-profit was absolutely outstanding, in all honesty. The free after-school therapy sessions, educational courses, and engaging experiential events like your firework shows and safari trips were/are all fantastic to me.

And to this day, I am so glad that a precious soul like yours seeked to create and lead something insanely special like this. I'm forever grateful to you, just like the children and families you have impacted through your work.

-

The authoritative clicks of a strong woman's heels continue to become louder... and louder...

-

I love my gifts... my genius... my creativity, and my dreams... blessings. I'm grateful for them all in more ways than I can ever express... but sometimes I hate myself. Well, maybe not myself, my brain. It's like a black hole living in there... a black hole that devoured infinity if that even makes sense. A creative... infinite... abyss.

A continual state of fireworks... the bright red, orange, and yellow flickers in the sky... painting an always new, unique, and unprecedented pattern each time... the various particles in the atmosphere falling as they lose their light... yet still so beautiful to the eye... it's attention-grabbing... grasping.

The booms... the crackles... the pops... so loud as they accompany one another until they fade out... their sound being lost in the night to be heard by no one again...

That's precisely how my brain is... as if there is a continual 4th of July celebration of ideas, wonder, and creation... never stopping... never sleeping.

What can I say though, when I'm the anomaly… nothing. But for that, I am grateful. Grateful that I can be special in this world… thankful that I was blessed to have you because I was special… even though I was never special enough to keep you.

We had countless conversations talking about how we could impact and change the world. Always debating on how best to show people that if you have vision and belief, you can change worlds and impact people's lives. Discussing the state of the world and how our brains work so elegantly and intricately in ways that we will never truly be able to comprehend.

And I know that you understand how I feel… what I'm saying… what goes on through my head. But despite the time, it always seemed as if our story was missing a piece of its puzzle, but I honestly just overlooked it. Maybe it was that I mistook it for another piece… I don't know.

What I do know, though, is that I am proud of you, Danielle.

Proud of you despite what we personally went through…

Proud of you despite the failures or shortcomings that you may have had along the way…

Proud of you for being authentically you…

And for that, I am grateful…

So get out there and do your thing for your show… I'll be watching from afar.

Be vulnerable… be true… be you… that was our promise…

Remember?

-

The dressing room door opens slowly, and she is greeted by an individual in all black saying calmly, "Honey, everyone is ready for you."

She opens her eyes, peering through the fog created by her tears, and looks at the exact book you're reading right now as she holds it in his right hand. A perfect-sized book… not too big… not too small. Not extremely daunting nor underwhelming. Gazing at the cover of this book, she reads,

But guess what…

I love me
I love who I am
I love who I was born to be
I love who I was destined to be
I love who I am fearlessly

This is My Burden Of Gratitude

His Burden Of Hope

Dove Park

To be the burden

To know a burden
To know how heavy a load things can be
To know how they can affect a person
To know how to deal with a burden

To see a burden
To see what damage it can inflict
To see what unbearable weight drags behind
To see what immense dream can be crushed

To be a burden
To be the creator of turmoil in a life
To be the reason a family has a strife
To be the reason another life has no light

To be the burden
To know a burden
To see a burden
To be a burden
And above all else
Try your hardest not
To be THE burden
The burden to all but you
Yet you are THE burden
The burden to none but you

Understand

Stop... Feel the book in your hands... its texture... its thickness... its lightweight. It's definitely lighter than the air currently surrounding you.

Wait, maybe not. Extend your arm forward and hold it there... straight forward... absolutely perpendicular to your body with your palm facing upwards. Hold the air... the air that is so weightless... the air that you walk through easily... the air that you inhale... exhale... so easily day in and day out.

Don't put your hand down. I need you to continue to hold the air that is deemed weightless by mankind.

Now understand that this story is about someone you love, care for, and cherish with all of your heart, mind, body, and soul. Somebody that you would sacrifice your own life for if it meant saving theirs. Imagine

their face… water slowly covering their eye, creating a glistening appearance… the water slowly collecting as if it is about to overflow… until the pool reaches its maximum capacity and each tear begins falling… slowly… ever so gently down their cheek… rolling down their face to be dropped and never seen again.

A burden just like the air. Weightless, while weight filled.

Tears filled with feelings. Full of emotion, too much to hold.

Feel his burden of Hope.

Self-Image's Refraction

What gives self-image its opacity?
See, self-image birthed opacity
But who birthed self-image?
Our image that was once unblemished and untouched
A valid question, some may say
Immaculate illumination through mediums
She is who births this image

A switch turned on and here comes the lights' pair
Lurking in the shadows,
accompanied by the absence of light,
Scared,
Flip the switch; here holds newfound voids of light
Now within the darkness lies its pair,
This light

Completely hidden out of sight

This fogs its transparency you see
Creating a new translucent object,
Try squinting; still, we can't really see

Obtaining clarity on this relationship is a dream
Improbably granted a true transparency
Why and who wholly unveiled
But light refracts, truthfully
The clouding medium which holds our image
Light and darkness blinding our once transparent image
Is what gives birth to this after-image
Regardless of patrilineage or matrilineage
This is what gives us our refracted self-image

But guess what...

I love me
I love who I am
I love who I was born to be
I love who I was destined to be
I love who I am gratefully

This is My Burden Of Hope

His
Burden Of
Intelligence

Prince Ocean

To be the burden

To know a burden
To know how heavy a load things can be
To know how they can affect a person
To know how to deal with a burden

To see a burden
To see what damage it can inflict
To see what unbearable weight drags behind
To see what immense dream can be crushed

To be a burden
To be the creator of turmoil in a life
To be the reason a family has a strife
To be the reason another life has no light

To be the burden
To know a burden
To see a burden
To be a burden
And above all else
Try your hardest not
To be THE burden
The burden to all but you
Yet you are THE burden
The burden to none but you

Understand

Stop… Feel the book in your hands… its texture… its thickness… its lightweight. It's definitely lighter than the air currently surrounding you.

Wait, maybe not. Extend your arm forward and hold it there… straight forward… absolutely perpendicular to your body with your palm facing upwards. Hold the air… the air that is so weightless… the air that you walk through easily… the air that you inhale… exhale… so easily day in and day out.

Don't put your hand down. I need you to continue to hold the air that is deemed weightless by mankind.

Now understand that this story is about someone you love, care for, and cherish with all of your heart, mind, body, and soul. Somebody that you would sacrifice your own life for if it meant saving theirs. Imagine

their face... water slowly covering their eye, creating a glistening appearance... the water slowly collecting as if it is about to overflow... until the pool reaches its maximum capacity. Each tear begins falling... slowly... ever so gently down their cheek... rolling down their face to be dropped and never seen again.

A burden just like the air. Weightless, while weight filled.

Tears filled with feelings. Full of emotion, too much to hold.

Feel his burden of Intelligence.

<u>Mahogany Teakwood</u>

The very essence of Mother Nature,

A tree… Solid, sturdy, and sound

Quite funny enough, it's all stuck – rooted in the ground…

Yet it sees more than most, but unphased it is

Now that there is power –

    Always unwavering, upright, tall

And on us, it won't fall

For that, there is trust, but no faith in us all

Chopped up and cut without regard

Built into buildings, then flames burned to tar

Until the precious histories these trees hold…

The faces they see…

The lives that they harbor…

And the world within thee…

All come to a finish…

Laid to rest with this tree

But guess what…

I love me
I love who I am
I love who I was born to be
I love who I was destined to be
I love who I am hopefully

This is My Burden Of Intelligence

His
Burden Of
Joviality

Leo Smalls

To be the burden

To know a burden
To know how heavy a load things can be
To know how they can affect a person
To know how to deal with a burden

To see a burden
To see what damage it can inflict
To see what unbearable weight drags behind
To see what immense dream can be crushed

To be a burden
To be the creator of turmoil in a life
To be the reason a family has a strife
To be the reason another life has no light

To be the burden
To know a burden
To see a burden
To be a burden
And above all else
Try your hardest not
To be THE burden
The burden to all but you
Yet you are THE burden
The burden to none but you

Understand

Stop... Feel the book in your hands... its texture... its thickness... its lightweight. It's definitely lighter than the air currently surrounding you.

Wait, maybe not. Extend your arm forward and hold it there... straight forward... absolutely perpendicular to your body with your palm facing upwards. Hold the air... the air that is so weightless... the air that you walk through easily... the air that you inhale... exhale... so easily day in and day out.

Don't put your hand down. I need you to continue to hold the air that is deemed weightless by mankind.

Now understand that this story is about someone you love, care for, and cherish with all of your heart, mind, body, and soul. Somebody that you would sacrifice your own life for if it meant saving theirs. Imagine

their face… water slowly covering their eye, creating a glistening appearance… the water slowly collecting as if it is about to overflow… until the pool reaches its maximum capacity. Each tear begins falling… slowly… ever so gently down their cheek… rolling down their face to be dropped and never seen again.

A burden just like the air. Weightless, while weight filled.

Tears filled with feelings. Full of emotion, too much to hold.

Feel his burden of Joviality.

Hotel Of Emotions

Part 1 - Greetings

Welcome to your stay,
In the Hotel Of Emotions
Are you simply here to enjoy
Or just go through the motions

Let me ponder a while,
Also, thanks for your greetings
My goal is to try and enjoy,
But my emotions have some meetings

Sure, I remember you, Sir
From the call on the phone
Seems you worked all the time
In a home, all alone

Told you to book a room ahead

Simply save yourself the time
But now to pay some extra
Robbed of being sublime

For that is true of my life
All alone with no wife
My hotel of emotions
Sliced with her knife

Meetings with these emotions
That's the last thing I want
Turned off all my feelings
In this hotel, they may haunt

Well, Sir, make the most of your stay
In this hotel of emotions
Attend your meetings every day
Don't just go through the motions

Part 2 - Your Itinerary

Visit one is with sadness
The aching, unpaid labor of love
Peace grounded like a flightless dove
Titled: How does one find true love?

On your left, that is madness
Perpetual battles – battlefield? – the mind
Rejecting the ones that you love
Titled: When will they know thereof?

Across from you, maybe badness
All your lies, grit, and terror
A never-ending battle of repair... trial-and-error
Titled: Wait, who's the bearer?

At the end there, that's gladness
Down past the sadness, madness, and badness
Guarding the door is a reflection of you
Titled: Who's really locked away your gladness?

Part 3 - The Key's Activation

So, enjoy your stay,
In the Hotel Of Emotions
Not to simply be here
Or just go through the motions

Ponder a while
Please try and enjoy
Attend all of your meetings
Be a man, not a boy

And next time, book ahead
No need for this dread
Take time for vacation
Whether it's in your head or even in your bed

For you should enjoy your vacations
Inhaling sweet aromas of colorful carnations
Never let your stay in the Hotel of Emotions
Singlehandedly destroy your foundations

But guess what…

I love me
I love who I am
I love who I was born to be
I love who I was destined to be
I love who I am intelligently

This is My Burden Of Joviality

His
Burden Of
Knowledge

Kay Ocean

To be the burden

To know a burden
To know how heavy a load things can be
To know how they can affect a person
To know how to deal with a burden

To see a burden
To see what damage it can inflict
To see what unbearable weight drags behind
To see what immense dream can be crushed

To be a burden
To be the creator of turmoil in a life
To be the reason a family has a strife
To be the reason another life has no light

To be the burden
To know a burden
To see a burden
To be a burden
And above all else
Try your hardest not
To be THE burden
The burden to all but you
Yet you are THE burden
The burden to none but you

Opening

opens box

"Mommy, I got a package," she exclaimed at the top of her lungs as she held the freshly opened box tightly to her chest, giving it a heartfelt hug.

While standing in front of her room door with her package, a smile grew across her face as if someone was pulling each cheek to stretch it to unnatural lengths. She was always excited and happy to get a package addressed to her, whether she knew what it was, who it was from, or what it was for. As long as she got a package and got to open it, it made her happier than a kid on Christmas day racing to their presents.

"I know, baby. I left it there for you because I knew that you would want nobody else to touch it," responded her mother from down the hall.

"Thanks, mommy," she exclaims back.

She slowly walks into her completely pink and blue bedroom, with stuffed animals ranging in size and species leaning against the walls of her room.

All the people that could have sent her this package race through her mind as she jumps stomach-first onto her favorite 8-foot pink, ever so soft, and fuzzy bean bag that her uncle had bought her years ago.

Looking down into her freshly opened cardboard box, she sees a book. A perfect-sized book... not too big... not too small. Not extremely daunting nor underwhelming. She sees the exact book you're reading right now, perfectly inside the small cardboard box she just opened up. Gazing at the cover of this book, she reads, "His Burden Of Knowledge."

Sitting up slightly, she yells to her mother, "Mom, are you or dad taking me to basketball practice today?"

When the sound hits her mother's ears, her mother softly responds, "Your dad will because I have a Zoom book club meeting tonight."

"Is grandma going to be there tonight, too," she asks.

"Yes, Kay. I'll tell her hello for you," her mother replies as she chuckles under her breath.

"Okay, thanks, mom! Tell dad I'll be ready to go soon," she exclaims in response to her mother.

Intrigued by the title, she opens the book.

opens book

Understand

Stop… Feel the book in your hands… its texture… its thickness… its lightweight. It's definitely lighter than the air currently surrounding you.

Wait, maybe not. Extend your arm forward and hold it there… straight forward… absolutely perpendicular to your body with your palm facing upwards. Hold the air… the air that is so weightless… the air that you walk through easily… the air that you inhale… exhale… so easily day in and day out.

Don't put your hand down. I need you to continue to hold the air that is deemed weightless by mankind.

Now understand that this story is about someone you love, care for, and cherish with all of your heart, mind, body, and soul. Somebody that you would sacrifice your own life for if it meant saving theirs. Imagine

their face... water slowly covering their eye, creating a glistening appearance... the water slowly collecting as if it is about to overflow... until the pool reaches its maximum capacity and each tear begins falling... slowly... ever so gently down their cheek... rolling down their face to be dropped and never seen again.

A burden just like the air. Weightless, while weight filled.

Tears filled with feelings. Full of emotion, too much to hold.

Feel his burden of Knowledge.

Start

Kay begins reading...

-

Hey, sunshine!

Speaking of sunshine, space... time... love... imagination... nature... everything is so interesting to me.

You know from all of the conversations that we had with your dad, Prince, right Kay? You used to always tell me that I overthink. You used to say I was your "nerdy uncle" and that I was weird but still cool. As long as I was something, though.

Speaking of me being a nerd, you have probably seen the news segments and magazines about me throughout these past years. I read those articles... watched those segments... each and every one of them, each and every day. They all talk about how I am a "genius." Like, what even is a genius?

"Exceptional intellectual or creative power or other natural ability"

How can I be a genius when I haven't even taken an IQ test… when I don't even know what the "I" and "Q" in IQ stand for?

Maybe I am more intelligent than most… maybe I am more creative… but maybe I got lucky and am here because of fate. That doesn't make me a genius, though. Does it?

-

Kay slowly sits up in her chair as if she just received life-changing news right before the beanbag envelopes her small 5' 2" body frame… causing her to succumb to its will and lay once again atop the pink beanbag.

-

I love to learn. However, what if this knowledge is what weighs me down… the countless thoughts that I have, chaining my thoughts to the intricacies of the universe… restraining me from grasping the time that I could've had with anyone else. Well, anything is better than being locked up alone with myself.

People don't know me. I fight to know everything but not even you truly know me, and you're my niece. Why is that... how come?

To care about learning... at least for me... isn't only about the book... it isn't solely about the knowledge I obtain while flipping through the pages of a dusty old textbook. The knowledge I cherish is about the world, and its people... about anyone and everyone throughout history and into the future. Everyone that has impacted my life in any fashion... I cherish that... I genuinely do. And I guess that I'm meant to be wrong for that. Go figure, a so-called "genius" is wrong for cherishing knowledge about others.

-

"I'm going to need some extra time to get ready for practice today, mom," says Kay as she tries to pull her broken voice back together through the tears.

-

And on top of that, I know that you haven't seen me in a while, but you never will again. I'm sorry... but you can't... for many reasons... countless reasons that I would love to explain but that you will never truly understand.

Currently, I'm on an island that I've been building for a long time now. That's why I haven't been in so many magazines or or TV lately, because I've been busy designing and logistically ensuring the execution of this lonely paradise. Anyway, there are so many animals, from chimpanzees, to axolotls, to deer, all roaming around the various ecosystems of the island. Like right now, I'm sitting in my lawn chair, and there are these birds flying above me so elegantly. I can hear a few monkeys playing together, the sounds of the tree branches bending and the crunches of the leaves as they swing from tree to tree chasing one another… they always do that. And sidenote, it was a pretty exciting story leading up to this, but I also just saw a hawk swoop down from the clouds and eat this tiny mouse. I honestly couldn't even explain how it all happened, but it was so wild to me.

That's beside the point, I'm sorry. Well, I say all that to say that you would love it here… well, anyone would really… but it's just me.

-

"Mom, I don't… I don't want to go to basketball practice today… anymore," says Kay as rivers flow down and off her deflated cheeks… dampening the fuzz that covers her favorite beanbag.

"What's wrong, sweetie? You were just so full of energy," her mother confusingly responds as she begins to make her way down the hall and to Kay's room, unbeknownst to Kay.

"Nothing," responds Kay as she wipes away the tears from her face with her left hand while simultaneously holding the book in her right hand.

-

Kay… you are a light in this world… you are a beautiful, blessed, and gifted child in this world… a truly special individual… and to me, a large influence in my "why." In this world where many people will try to dim your light, you must keep fighting and seek to understand other people's perspectives.

"Learn, teach, educate."

So, please learn all you can and be the change you want in this world, Kay. You can do it, and I love you… my oh-so-amazing niece.

To be able to exude positive energy, radiate light in this world, is something that is hard to achieve but even harder to maintain as life progresses. But, the fact that you have been able to keep your light shining, despite whatever is going on in the entire world, is absolutely amazing. And that's why I've always called you my precious little Sun… because just like the Sun, you make everybody's day brighter the second you rise every day. So keep that, Kay… continue being the light that warms the hearts of the numerous hearts in the world… and never let your light dim for anybody… anything… because you are enough… you are special… you are terrific… and I love you, sunshine.

-

Kay's mother walks into the room, and her eyes fixate upon her daughter… sunken into the pink beanbag that her brother brought her daughter several years ago. All alone, Kay sits sobbing… quietly… with her poor little hands shaking from anxiety… her heart racing.

Kay slowly looks up from her book and locks eyes with her mother, and tears begin to build up in the crevices of her eyes. Then, almost as if the lock of their eyes gave Kay permission to let out all of her emotions, her head falls back, her eyes close, and she begins to weep.

Her mother runs over to Kay and holds her tight in her arms, while rocking her back and forth like she is trying to rock a baby to sleep. She calmly and comfortingly whispers with her soothing voice in Kay's ear, "It's okay, baby. Whatever it is... it is truly okay. Trust me, Kay... trust me... I know that it will all be okay."

She opens her eyes, peering through the fog created by her tears, and looks at the same book you're reading right now as she holds it in her right hand. A perfect-sized book... not too big... not too small. Not extremely daunting nor underwhelming. Gazing at the cover of this book, she reads,

But guess what…

I love me
I love who I am
I love who I was born to be
I love who I was destined to be
I love who I am jovially

This is My Burden Of Knowledge

His
Burden Of
Love

Viola Race

To be the burden

To know a burden
To know how heavy a load things can be
To know how they can affect a person
To know how to deal with a burden

To see a burden
To see what damage it can inflict
To see what unbearable weight drags behind
To see what immense dream can be crushed

To be a burden
To be the creator of turmoil in a life
To be the reason a family has a strife
To be the reason another life has no light

To be the burden
To know a burden
To see a burden
To be a burden
And above all else
Try your hardest not
To be THE burden
The burden to all but you
Yet you are THE burden
The burden to none but you

Opening

opens box

The Sun beams in from the perfectly placed window that sits in the center of the yellow-painted wall to her left... not a cloud in the sky... no chance of rain. This here is a simply magnificent sight to wake up to each and every morning before rolling out of bed.

Almost as if moving in slow motion, she rises up from the comfort of her memory foam mattress... her back leaving the delicate feeling of the gray silk sheets. Following suit, the weighted blanket that holds her tight and her flower-patterned comforter slowly slide down her knees.

"Another one-night stand to start off the week... not anything that ever stays anyway," she says to herself.

Taking in a deep breath, her chest slowly inflates, creating the slightest arch in her back... an arch that continues to grow as she stretches and inhales what seems to be all of the oxygen in the room.

Looking down into her freshly opened cardboard box, she sees a book. A perfect-sized book... not too big...

not too small. Not extremely daunting nor underwhelming. She sees the exact book you're reading right now, lying perfectly inside the small cardboard box she just opened. Gazing at the cover of this book, she reads, "His Burden Of Love."

A tear slowly streams down the right side of her face… getting down no further than the bottom of her soft, plump lips before she hurriedly wipes the tear away with urgency. It's almost like she's attempting to hide the tear from someone. Instead, however, she is all alone, sitting atop her bed, hiding her tears from herself for reasons unknown.

"Love… if only," she says to herself before swinging her legs off the left side of her bed.

She looks through the blurred lenses of her two teary eyes and reads the yellow poster that holds her favorite quote in bold-white letters sitting directly across from her bed,

"You Are Special

You Are Enough

You Are Loved."

Her light brown toes... followed by the bottoms of her soft, brown feet... slowly sink into the soft, 2-inch layer of fur that makes up the plush, white rug as she steps off of the bed.

She takes four steps toward the window that showcases the art of her developing city. The bluebirds, small enough to sit in the cupped hands of a human, sing to the surrounding world ever so beautifully. Ever so slightly, the wind blows, creating the gentle ruffle of the countless tree leaves. The subtle sounds of the children's laughs that are playing in the park, swinging on the dark green swing set, and sliding down the bright yellow slide, fill the playground below.

It's a masterpiece to her... a masterpiece so beautiful and intricate as it continually evolves every day. Each development organized through her various non-profits gets added to her home city month after month, year after year.

"Love... tell me about it," she says as she holds the book out in front of her... the pages illuminated by the Sun.

opens book

Understand

Stop… Feel the book in your hands… its texture… its thickness… its lightweight. It's definitely lighter than the air currently surrounding you.

Wait, maybe not. Extend your arm forward and hold it there… straight forward… absolutely perpendicular to your body with your palm facing upwards. Hold the air… the air that is so weightless… the air that you walk through easily… the air that you inhale… exhale… so easily day in and day out.

Don't put your hand down. I need you to continue to hold the air that is deemed weightless by mankind.

Now understand that this story is about someone you love, care for, and cherish with all of your heart, mind, body, and soul. Somebody that you would sacrifice your own life for if it meant saving theirs. Imagine

their face... water slowly covering their eye, creating a glistening appearance... the water slowly collecting as if it is about to overflow... until the pool reaches its maximum capacity. Each tear begins falling... slowly... ever so gently down their cheek... rolling down their face to be dropped and never seen again.

A burden just like the air. Weightless, while weight filled.

Tears filled with feelings. Full of emotion, too much to hold.

Feel his burden of Love.

Start

Viola begins reading…

-

Hello love… "love"… that four-letter word everyone treasures so deeply… that can create a feeling of pure belonging… happiness… joy. True love. Soulmates.

That's what I believed we were… from the moment we met. Do you remember? Because I could never forget it. You made me feel like nobody else in my life has ever made me feel, Viola… comfortable like no one else ever could… happy like no one else ever would.

So, I always wonder now, why? Why did it have to end? Why did we ever fall in love so deeply? Why did you tell me you felt as I did and then leave me in the end… when if you genuinely felt like me, you would have never?

-

Viola looks up again at the masterpiece that has evolved yet again in the short amount of time it took her to read the beginning of her message.

Her eyes slowly fall back down at the book as a look of sadness persists to fall upon her face.

-

I remember that call like it was yesterday… when I knew it was entirely over. You were on your way, and you forcefully sent me on mine. But, even still, I never forgot what we shared. From the moments walking through the botanical gardens, to the dates that we had at our favorite restaurants, all of the way to the countless hours that we spent looking up at the stars… the bright, little stars that lit up the night sky… I never forgot. I'll always remember it. As I always do… I will always remember.

I'm not saying that it halts me… stops me from what I need to do in life, or distracts me from where I need to go, but I do think about you… about love. And maybe it's because I cherish this thing that we call "love" too much. I give too much of myself to the world, to the people that I truly care about, even when their season in my life has passed. Love… I take it to heart… And therefore, I love… and with this unconditionality… vulnerability… comes an immeasurable space for pain.

I get hurt time and time again for pouring my love out to the world… and all for what? Is it because, deep down,

I'm longing for the same love back? Will I ever be truly loved back… ever more than I love another? Of course, that is what I want, but it doesn't seem like it will ever happen… for someone's love for me to outweigh my love for them.

This may be how it was meant to be. But, I'll be okay with it never happening because perhaps I have to bear this weight since no one else can.

-

Viola's head slowly shakes from the left… and to the right… slowly back and forth as if she is trying to convince herself that what she is reading is not true at all.

-

Some years ago, Viola, I started building this island. It's fully self-sustaining. It has everything that I ever wanted (including that infinity pool that overlooks the beautiful horizon that we always talked about getting). Honestly, it is truly magnificent… a true masterpiece.

The ocean is breathtaking, with clear blue water, just like you loved when we used to go on vacation. And yes, this does sound amazing, and it really is. It's just that I'm the only one here... not by choice... indirectly by force, it seems. It feels like I had to, as it was the only option after I tried so hard to find someone like me... someone who loved me... connected with me the same way I did with them.

Even after I felt like giving up on connection and love... I really couldn't. Romanticizing over the endless possibilities that these feelings can hold and evolve into... with close friends... now distant acquaintances... even strangers.

I love to do it even though it always hurts in the end. I always paint a vivid picture of what could be and what it feels like should be... but it never matches how it truly turns out to be.

-

Tears continue racing down each one of Viola's deflated brown cheeks as her eyes remain focused on her book.

-

And no, I never wanted there to be anything fake… no fake love… no fake care… no fake support… nor anything of the sort. I just sometimes wish that it was all different… that the same love I have in my heart and soul… that someone else in this vast and expansive world can replicate or even outmatch that… but I don't know if that is possible.

And even though that is not possible… that we didn't work out the way we always laughed and talked about… the way I found my form of peace with it all was in self-love, and I hope that you can find that too. The love for yourself that is unconditional, unwavering, and unchanging no matter what happens. No matter what tribulations you must endure or other people's perspectives of you, I need you to always know that you are enough and do as well deserve love. So, love yourself, and I truly pray that you find someone that loves you as much as I. All good things, Viola… all good things.

-

In its biggest evolution yet, the window's masterpiece sitting before Viola begins to exude more meaning than ever before. It begins to invoke more emotion as she fully processes and remembers how this masterpiece came to be… who it was that helped her

revive her hometown... upgrade her quality of life... change the lives of the people of every community that she touched.

"I love you... and I'm so sorry," Viola uttered silently as her head dropped once again... her blunt chin forcefully connecting with her chest... causing her body to bounce with every sob that she quietly let out... all alone in her room.

Yet, she opens her eyes, slowly peering through the fog created by her tears, and looks at the same book you're reading right now as she holds it in her right hand. A perfect-sized book... not too big... not too small. Not extremely daunting nor underwhelming. Gazing at the cover of this book, she reads,

But guess what…

I love me
I love who I am
I love who I was born to be
I love who I was destined to be
I love who I am knowledgeably

This is My Burden Of Love

His
Burden Of
Magnanimity

Fatimah Morris

To be the burden

To know a burden
To know how heavy a load things can be
To know how they can affect a person
To know how to deal with a burden

To see a burden
To see what damage it can inflict
To see what unbearable weight drags behind
To see what immense dream can be crushed

To be a burden
To be the creator of turmoil in a life
To be the reason a family has a strife
To be the reason another life has no light

To be the burden
To know a burden
To see a burden
To be a burden
And above all else
Try your hardest not
To be THE burden
The burden to all but you
Yet you are THE burden
The burden to none but you

Understand

Stop... Feel the book in your hands... its texture... its thickness... its lightweight. It's definitely lighter than the air currently surrounding you.

Wait, maybe not. Extend your arm forward and hold it there... straight forward... absolutely perpendicular to your body with your palm facing upwards. Hold the air... the air that is so weightless... the air that you walk through easily... the air that you inhale... exhale... so easily day in and day out.

Don't put your hand down. I need you to continue to hold the air that is deemed weightless by mankind.

Now understand that this story is about someone you love, care for, and cherish with all of your heart, mind, body, and soul. Somebody that you would sacrifice your own life for if it meant saving theirs. Imagine

their face... water slowly covering their eye, creating a glistening appearance... the water slowly collecting as if it is about to overflow... until the pool reaches its maximum capacity and each tear begins falling... slowly... ever so gently down their cheek... rolling down their face to be dropped and never seen again.

A burden just like the air. Weightless, while weight filled.

Tears filled with feelings. Full of emotion, too much to hold.

Feel his burden of Magnanimity.

<u>My Peace</u>

Downtrodden, broken-hearted
The last puzzle piece of a heart lost
Now, I am journeying across the sea to find it
Steadily gathering roses, lilies, tulips
Painted in the finest flamingo pink

Lost all alone as I roam
Understanding it's truly all for naught
Forging a path
For which you are the last
You are my one piece

But guess what…

I love me
I love who I am
I love who I was born to be
I love who I was destined to be
I love who I am lovingly

This is My Burden Of Magnanimity

His
Burden Of
Nourishment

Steel Jackson

To be the burden

To know a burden

To know how heavy a load things can be
To know how they can affect a person
To know how to deal with a burden

To see a burden

To see what damage it can inflict
To see what unbearable weight drags behind
To see what immense dream can be crushed

To be a burden

To be the creator of turmoil in a life
To be the reason a family has a strife
To be the reason another life has no light

To be the burden

To know a burden
To see a burden
To be a burden
And above all else
Try your hardest not
To be THE burden
The burden to all but you
Yet you are THE burden
The burden to none but you

Understand

Stop... Feel the book in your hands... its texture... its thickness... its lightweight. It's definitely lighter than the air currently surrounding you.

Wait, maybe not. Extend your arm forward and hold it there... straight forward... absolutely perpendicular to your body with your palm facing upwards. Hold the air... the air that is so weightless... the air that you walk through easily... the air that you inhale... exhale... so easily day in and day out.

Don't put your hand down. I need you to continue to hold the air that is deemed weightless by mankind.

Now understand that this story is about someone you love, care for, and cherish with all of your heart, mind, body, and soul. Somebody that you would sacrifice your own life for if it meant saving theirs. Imagine

their face... water slowly covering their eye, creating a glistening appearance... the water slowly collecting as if it is about to overflow... until the pool reaches its maximum capacity and each tear begins falling... slowly... ever so gently down their cheek... rolling down their face to be dropped and never seen again.

A burden just like the air. Weightless, while weight filled.

Tears filled with feelings. Full of emotion, too much to hold.

Feel his burden of Nourishment.

The World's Halitosis

This cold metal tank is my residence
My home is where I inhale this gas
Pouring in and filling each of my lungs
So careful not to shatter this glass

Toxic gas from the doubters
Nourishing this glass of mine
Toxicity spewed from them to me
"Don't shine, don't be fine"

My entire body toxic
Completely surrounded by gas
This will surely mark my end
I bet then they'll shout, "Alas"

"Oh, this smell is appalling"
And I hear yet another clang
"Man, I wish this was the end"
"Well, sir, now it is" - *BANG*

But guess what…

I love me
I love who I am
I love who I was born to be
I love who I was destined to be
I love who I am magnanimously

This is My Burden Of Nourishment

His
Burden Of
Opportunities

Sita Ocean

To be the burden

To know a burden
To know how heavy a load things can be
To know how they can affect a person
To know how to deal with a burden

To see a burden
To see what damage it can inflict
To see what unbearable weight drags behind
To see what immense dream can be crushed

To be a burden
To be the creator of turmoil in a life
To be the reason a family has a strife
To be the reason another life has no light

To be the burden
To know a burden
To see a burden
To be a burden
And above all else
Try your hardest not
To be THE burden
The burden to all but you
Yet you are THE burden
The burden to none but you

Understand

Stop... Feel the book in your hands... its texture... its thickness... its lightweight. It's definitely lighter than the air currently surrounding you.

Wait, maybe not. Extend your arm forward and hold it there... straight forward... absolutely perpendicular to your body with your palm facing upwards. Hold the air... the air that is so weightless... the air that you walk through easily... the air that you inhale... exhale... so easily day in and day out.

Don't put your hand down. I need you to continue to hold the air that is deemed weightless by mankind.

Now understand that this story is about someone you love, care for, and cherish with all of your heart, mind, body, and soul. Somebody that you would sacrifice your own life for if it meant saving theirs. Imagine

their face... water slowly covering their eye, creating a glistening appearance... the water slowly collecting as if it is about to overflow... until the pool reaches its maximum capacity and each tear begins falling... slowly... ever so gently down their cheek... rolling down their face to be dropped and never seen again.

A burden just like the air. Weightless, while weight filled.

Tears filled with feelings. Full of emotion, too much to hold.

Feel his burden of Opportunities.

<u>Tempo</u>

What to do with all this time?

My formidably harsh paradigm

A subtle paradox twisting,

    in this mind of mine

Creations mountain – Oh! the most sublime

They tell us, "Keep Your Tempo,

    and follow the line"

But guess what…

I love me
I love who I am
I love who I was born to be
I love who I was destined to be
I love who I am nourishingly

This is My Burden Of Opportunities

His
Burden Of
Power

Wade Clark

To be the burden

To know a burden
To know how heavy a load things can be
To know how they can affect a person
To know how to deal with a burden

To see a burden
To see what damage it can inflict
To see what unbearable weight drags behind
To see what immense dream can be crushed

To be a burden
To be the creator of turmoil in a life
To be the reason a family has a strife
To be the reason another life has no light

To be the burden
To know a burden
To see a burden
To be a burden
And above all else
Try your hardest not
To be THE burden
The burden to all but you
Yet you are THE burden
The burden to none but you

Opening

opens box

A metal sign hanging on the brown wooden door standing before him reads,

"Welcome To The Wade Clark Entertainment Center"

Gripping the cold, golden doorknob with his left hand... holding this box in his right hand... he slowly opens the door.

As he walks inside the room, he sees the red walls of the room slightly illuminated by the dim, white LED lights that line the corners of the ceiling. In his quick scan of the room, he sees four of his friends, each sitting on a black barstool at the bar. As he continues his scan, he sees three of his friends sitting on the long, brown leather couch watching TV on the 8-foot-wide screen in the far-left corner. Lastly, he sees six of his friends in the arcade area, which occupies the right side of the room.

"WADE," all of his friends exclaim as they turn and see him standing in the doorway.

"What's up y'all! It's been too long," Wade responds as he takes a few more steps into the room, all before shutting the door gently behind himself.

At the center of the room sits a dark chocolate-colored mahogany pool table with soft, green felt lining the surface. The legs of the table had images carved in them... hand-carved illustrations by Wade himself symbolizing his deep African roots.

He loves this table as it is his prized possession. This precious, tangible object holds so many precious, intangible memories. Little does he know, another memory is about to be made... a moment he will never forget.

Wade greets his various friends before making his way to the center of the room alongside another occupant. When the two men reach the center of the room, they each grab their pool sticks, Wade grabbing his own lucky pool stick, and begin to set up the game.

As the pool balls are being racked by his opponent in the conventional triangle formation, Wade remembers his package.

Looking down into his freshly opened cardboard box, he sees a book. A perfect-sized book... not too big... not too small. Not extremely daunting nor underwhelming. He sees the exact book you're reading right now lying perfectly inside the small cardboard box he just opened. Gazing at the cover of this book, he reads, "His Burden Of Power."

"Run it," says Wade as he looks back down at the book sitting on the mahogany pool table.

"Don't get too confident now, Mr. Clark," his opponent responds jokingly before lining up his first shot.

As his friend takes his shot, Wade hears the announcer's deep, booming voice exclaim through the television, "Welcome to the stage for her FINAL performance for the world, MRS. KARA PLAID!"

opens book

Understand

Stop... Feel the book in your hands... its texture... its thickness... its lightweight. It's definitely lighter than the air currently surrounding you.

Wait, maybe not. Extend your arm forward and hold it there... straight forward... absolutely perpendicular to your body with your palm facing upwards. Hold the air... the air that is so weightless... the air that you walk through easily... the air that you inhale... exhale... so easily day in and day out.

Don't put your hand down. I need you to continue to hold the air that is deemed weightless by mankind.

Now understand that this story is about someone you love, care for, and cherish with all of your heart, mind, body, and soul. Somebody that you would sacrifice your own life for if it meant saving theirs. Imagine

their face... water slowly covering their eye, creating a glistening appearance... the water slowly collecting as if it is about to overflow... until the pool reaches its maximum capacity. Each tear begins falling... slowly... ever so gently down their cheek... rolling down their face to be dropped and never seen again.

A burden just like the air. Weightless, while weight filled.

Tears filled with feelings. Full of emotion, too much to hold.

Feel his burden of Power.

Start

Wade begins reading…

-

My brother… joined by love and bond… yet not by blood, but by adventures, laughs, triumphs… precious memories. I genuinely hope that you've been well and have been pursuing your passions… ambitions… dreams.

Now, I know that we haven't talked in some time. I don't know why or how, but ever since you moved, it seemed like you became distant, but the love for you is still there. We grew up together… got through our darkest lows together… celebrated our most significant victories together.

I remember playing basketball in high school and being two-time state champions in our junior and senior years… hooping as if our lives depended on it. I enjoyed the extra practice time, film reviews, celebrations, & conversations that came alongside the journey to us winning those championships.

Pool club back in college… do you remember that man? I remember when you brought it up to me… about joining…

since we had to join a club. I even remembe and how terrible we were at first. Good times man... great times, actually. And then the custom carving business that you started with you ending up designing that pool table for your crib. Oh yeah, and that mahogany door for the Zhuri's mansion some years ago. Thanks again for that too, man.

And maybe it sounds like I'm saying thank you a lot... it feels like I'm writing it a lot. It's just that I really don't know if I ever thanked you for all of that... if I ever truly let you know how appreciative I am of what you did for me... with me... that we were able to journey through life together as best friends. I truly cherish the fact that somehow our lives got connected, and I was able to have another brother.

-

A mixture of emotions radiates throughout Wade's body as he realizes who this message is from. Unfortunately, these emotions put Wade a little bit off his game as he misses an easy shot after knocking in a couple of striped balls.

Wade continues reading as he walks to the bar to get a drink before returning to the table.

-

We had so much ambition, big dreams, and goals that we wanted to accomplish… impacts that we wanted to make on the world.

And as you know, wasted potential is what I despise the most in this world. When people are blessed with gifts that can change the world and impact the lives of others, but then they don't use them for those reasons. They don't follow their true passions and dreams because they are living for somebody else… wanting to fit in with the norm… being too lazy to put in the time and work to be great. It utterly irks me to my core.

And maybe that's just me being judgemental... On the other hand, it could be just me being self-centered… egotistical… narcissistic… thinking everyone can do what I can. Why can't they, though… when anything is possible?

Like you… I believe in you and everything that you do. I support you in every move you make, and I'll never let you feel alone or that you have no support in your career. Deep down though… I feel like I failed you.

-

Wade's face slowly fades into a blank stare, and he begins to move around the table almost as if he's a robot… completely locked in to the game. Then, with what seems like a sort of urgency, he begins perfectly lining up shots, taking them without hesitation.

He knocks in four more balls, each into their own individual pocket, before he begins to line up his final striped ball shot… and he misses.

Then, Wade begins to read again.

-

Is it wrong to say that I am disappointed? Disappointed in you for not igniting the pure happiness and joy that are your ancestors' that you treasure so much… their wildest dreams. Disappointed in me because I still believe that you can do what I can do… just in your own way.

And through my life, I have learned that everyone is different and that I am an anomaly among that difference. I want to be the greatest in all aspects of life, creating a world that is better for everyone now and in the future. But everyone doesn't want to be that, and I don't know if I will ever fully understand… if I will ever be able to truly accept it.

But I won't press it, and that is why I am here… alone… hoping and praying that somehow, someway, I can help people live the lives of their dreams… especially people that I love like you, Wade.

Right now, I'm on this island that I've been designing for the past number of years. It's fully self-sustaining with all sorts of exotic fruits and vegetables, land and marine life, and luscious vegetation. It genuinely looks like it's out of a dream. I have multiple ATV courses that run through the deep deciduous forest covering many acres of the island and across the flawless beach with water so clear that you can see your toes when you look down. I also have a pool table that I plan to practice my game on sometimes. I even have both indoor and outdoor basketball courts… ones I still haven't been able to put up a single shot on, but that you would love too. You would love it here… well, anyone would really… but I'm the only one.

-

Taken aback, Wade attempts to line up his shot again, but he uncharacteristically misses again.

"You've been playing pool for ages now, Wade. So, don't try and play with me now or go easy on me 'cause you will most definitely lose," says Wade's opponent.

-

You know how I'm all over the place when I'm talking… going on about this and that, but you know what I'm trying to say. And I genuinely hope that you are somewhat happy to hear from your old friend again. Happy in your life… following your dreams and not being complacent…utilizing your power of potential… living for yourself and not for others… living and being at peace with life. Use that power of yours carefully and to the fullest potential.

I love you, brother. And I pray that you… your wife… you children… everybody in your family is staying happy and healthy, Wade.

-

Wade attempts to hit his final striped ball in, but his angle is off… misaligned slightly to the right causing the cue ball to bounce off the perpendicular sides of the corner pocket's walls. Accompanied by the

overcompensating amount of power that he struck the ball with, the cue ball's momentum continues forward... approaching the ostracized ball.

He and his opponent slowly watch as the cue ball continues to roll... losing momentum with each passing second... until it strikes the lone, black ball sitting right outside of a pocket. The ricocheted ball slowly rolls toward the pocket until it becomes motionless in its final resting place.

Wade feels his heart become heavy as emotion begins engulfing and almost overflowing from his body... almost as if his heart has a pocket in the center of it... about 4.5 inches wide... perfect for a 2 3/8 inch wide ball.

Wade opens his eyes, peering through the fog created by his tears, and looks at the same book you're reading right now as he holds it in his right hand. A perfect-sized book... not too big... not too small. Not extremely daunting nor underwhelming. Gazing at the cover of this book, he reads,

But guess what…

I love me
I love who I am
I love who I was born to be
I love who I was destined to be
I love who I am opportunistically

This is My Burden Of Power

His
Burden Of
Quaintness

Scarlet Love

To be the burden

To know a burden
To know how heavy a load things can be
To know how they can affect a person
To know how to deal with a burden

To see a burden
To see what damage it can inflict
To see what unbearable weight drags behind
To see what immense dream can be crushed

To be a burden
To be the creator of turmoil in a life
To be the reason a family has a strife
To be the reason another life has no light

To be the burden
To know a burden
To see a burden
To be a burden
And above all else
Try your hardest not
To be THE burden
The burden to all but you
Yet you are THE burden
The burden to none but you

Opening

This woman is Scarlet... Scarlet Love... the world-renowned artist, wife, and mother of two beautiful young girls. And this very room she sits in right now is her favorite room to occupy... the room that brings her the most peace... joy... and happiness when she needs it the most.

Sitting on the white tile floor at the center of a room, with all-white walls surrounding her & various colorful works of art covering the walls, is a beautiful dark-skinned woman with long, dark brown knotless braids running down her back. And on her chest sits the face of Leo Smalls on her cold, white t-shirt... on her back, a poem reading, "You Are Special, You Are Enough, You Are Loved."

Surrounding here are these beautiful abstract paintings, with colors colliding and intertwining into extraordinary works of art, hung upon the wall sitting directly behind her.

On the wall to her right are incredibly imaginative depictions of the natural and mythical worlds merging into one... the animals and creatures interacting with one another in a world unknown to us.

Quaint, old-fashioned baroque and renaissance works fill the wall to her left, while directly in front of her sits a blank wall. This empty wall is for a mural that she has been hesitating about working on for the past couple of weeks.

opens box

Goosebumps slowly rise from her skin, perfectly on cue with the simultaneous opening of her box.

Looking down into her freshly opened cardboard box, she sees a book. A perfect-sized book... not too big... not too small. Not extremely daunting nor underwhelming. She sees the exact book you're reading right now, lying perfectly inside the small cardboard box she just opened. Gazing at the cover of this book, she reads, "His Burden Of Quaintness."

As she takes a deep breath, she closes her eyes to maximize the calming effect of her breathing. She listens to herself inhale... and exhale... hearing the blood pump from her heart... feeling the blood flow throughout her arteries and veins... until the blood once again reaches her heart, deoxygenated, just to start the entire cycle over again.

"You got this," Scarlet says to herself.

opens book

Understand

Stop... Feel the book in your hands... its texture... its thickness... its lightweight. It's definitely lighter than the air currently surrounding you.

Wait, maybe not. Extend your arm forward and hold it there... straight forward... absolutely perpendicular to your body with your palm facing upwards. Hold the air... the air that is so weightless... the air that you walk through easily... the air that you inhale... exhale... so easily day in and day out.

Don't put your hand down. I need you to continue to hold the air that is deemed weightless by mankind.

Now understand that this story is about someone you love, care for, and cherish with all of your heart, mind, body, and soul. Somebody that you would sacrifice your own life for if it meant saving theirs. Imagine

their face... water slowly covering their eye, creating a glistening appearance... the water slowly collecting as if it is about to overflow... until the pool reaches its maximum capacity and each tear begins falling... slowly... ever so gently down their cheek... rolling down their face to be dropped and never seen again.

A burden just like the air. Weightless, while weight filled.

Tears filled with feelings. Full of emotion, too much to hold.

Feel his burden of Quaintness.

Scarlet begins reading…

-

Hey, Scarlet. I don't know how to open this up, so I just wanted to say hello and thank you for everything that you are to this world… to me… to everyone.

I believe that we all evolve with each person we come across… that we all take things away from every individual we interact with… from every moment we experience.

I sort of relate it to art… it's why I love your art and have been mesmerized by it ever since I saw your first piece of work… each one with your signature… signed "Scarlet Love."

The beautiful art that you create ever so carefully, with no mistakes, brings me so many joys, new perspectives, and understandings of this world we live in. In a way, your art is almost the perfect analogy of life.

If I had to describe it to you, it is like adding strokes to a masterpiece… all starting when you're born as a child… you start off as a completely blank canvas.

-

Raising her head slowly from her book, she looks straight ahead at the blank wall... her utterly blank canvas.

Scarlet slowly begins to stand up... pushing up on the cold, white tile floor with her free hand... until she is standing facing the blank canvas in front of her.

She takes a few steps toward the wall until it is about 15 feet away, and then her gaze slowly fixates back upon the book.

-

We each pick up a paintbrush unknowingly, and we begin to paint on our blank canvas with the help of others. Whether good or bad... we begin our canvas.

As time passes and we begin to grow older, this dynamic begins to shift as we take control of our lives... opinions... perspectives for ourselves as we learn to navigate through life.

We add strokes with each moment that could be any color on the entire spectrum of the rainbow. Further progressing through life, various tools and brushes are added to our different collections that we can use to help shape our canvas.

And of course, everyone makes mistakes, has bad experiences, runs into bad people... but these strokes don't mean disaster for the elegant, happiness-filled strokes.

But even though these strokes were covered up, it doesn't mean that they are non-existent... it doesn't mean that they never happened. They're just masked or covered up by maybe another person or experience so that they aren't at the forefront of your painting... your masterpiece... your life.

Sometimes, some of the paint would fade away... wear down... become a pentimento, revealing the negative occurrences that happened throughout life.

But it has truly been people like you that have come into my life, even if it was only for a season or a reason, that has kept my masterpiece beautiful. I am me because of you and everything we have shared throughout life, and I genuinely appreciate everything from you for that.

-

Scarlet leaves the art room and retrieves supplies from her supply closet right outside the room.

-

And I believe that the craziest part about life is that the viewpoint that is taken upon one's situation is how one will view the world and their situation... just like art.

No matter what, based off of each and every person's various experiences... along with all of the people that they come across... on top of that, their own situation and the situations of people close to them... they will each have a different subjective view on the art placed before them. That's what makes art so beautiful to me... that is what makes life so beautiful to me.

Based on my canvas, I decided to construct an island. I enjoy the heat, so it is purposefully near the equator so that I can enjoy myself and the tropical nature that I love so much. There are these jet-black birds flying, large and small snakes, little gray and brown mice, brown and black hawks, white-tailed deer, and everything in between. A few minutes ago, one of those hawks that I was just talking about dove down to get a mouse that it saw for lunch, which was absolutely insane too.

I love it... the nature... the peace... the life around me... and that is why I am alone here. Of course, it would be better with others... with precious friends and family to enjoy this paradise with... make memories with... share laughs with... but that isn't an option.

-

After a few minutes of retrieving various items such as her favorite brushes, tubes of paint, correctors, and various other tools, she re-enters the art room... standing once again before the blank, white wall.

-

I also don't necessarily know how to end this off either, but I just always need you to know that finding and choosing to share your magical love... joy... happiness with someone... can mean the world to them.

People like you in this world are what is needed... People like you are required in order to add beautiful strokes across everyone's masterpiece of life. So keep being the oh, so special you, Scarlet.

-

Once seemingly set on finally starting on the canvas that she has been meaning to work on for some time, Scarlet's body begins to numb…

Cold tears begin to run down her plump, dark-brown cheeks as her body overcomes with emotion.   Slowly spinning around 360 degrees, her gaze fixates on each one of the various paintings hanging on the walls.

She struggles as she attempts to focus on each of them… with the harder she tries to concentrate, the more that the paintings in her peripherals begin to blur out until the images run together in a deep haze.

After completing her revolution, she once again stares ahead of her… a completely untouched canvas… right before looking down at her inflated mid-section… feeling a slight push coming from inside… more accurately, a kick… soon to be another untouched canvas.

She then opens her eyes, peering through the fog created by her tears, and looks at the exact book you're reading right now as she holds it in her right hand. A perfect-sized book... not too big... not too small. Not extremely daunting nor underwhelming.

Gazing at the cover of this book, she reads,

But guess what…

I love me
I love who I am
I love who I was born to be
I love who I was destined to be
I love who I am powerfully

This is My Burden Of Quaintness

His Burden Of Respect

Cleo Thorne

To be the burden

To know a burden
To know how heavy a load things can be
To know how they can affect a person
To know how to deal with a burden

To see a burden
To see what damage it can inflict
To see what unbearable weight drags behind
To see what immense dream can be crushed

To be a burden
To be the creator of turmoil in a life
To be the reason a family has a strife
To be the reason another life has no light

To be the burden
To know a burden
To see a burden
To be a burden
And above all else
Try your hardest not
To be THE burden
The burden to all but you
Yet you are THE burden
The burden to none but you

Understand

Stop... Feel the book in your hands... its texture... its thickness... its lightweight. It's definitely lighter than the air currently surrounding you.

Wait, maybe not. Extend your arm forward and hold it there... straight forward... absolutely perpendicular to your body with your palm facing upwards. Hold the air... the air that is so weightless... the air that you walk through easily... the air that you inhale... exhale... so easily day in and day out.

Don't put your hand down. I need you to continue to hold the air that is deemed weightless by mankind.

Now understand that this story is about someone you love, care for, and cherish with all of your heart, mind, body, and soul. Somebody that you would sacrifice your own life for if it meant saving theirs. Imagine

their face… water slowly covering their eye, creating a glistening appearance… the water slowly collecting as if it is about to overflow… until the pool reaches its maximum capacity. Each tear begins falling… slowly… ever so gently down their cheek… rolling down their face to be dropped and never seen again.

A burden just like the air. Weightless, while weight filled.

Tears filled with feelings. Full of emotion, too much to hold.

Feel his burden of Respect.

<u>You</u>

What makes you… You?

That word won't ever mean to me,

What it could ever mean to you

Fluid in its each and every use

Together — when speaking of we

Harmony — when speaking of you and I

Yet you see it as You & i

And Why? – I Owe You?

… So I ask you,

What makes you, You…

And me, your i?

But guess what…

I love me
I love who I am
I love who I was born to be
I love who I was destined to be
I love who I am quaintly

This is My Burden Of Respect

His
Burden Of
Support

Lexi Jones

To be the burden

To know a burden
To know how heavy a load things can be
To know how they can affect a person
To know how to deal with a burden

To see a burden
To see what damage it can inflict
To see what unbearable weight drags behind
To see what immense dream can be crushed

To be a burden
To be the creator of turmoil in a life
To be the reason a family has a strife
To be the reason another life has no light

To be the burden
To know a burden
To see a burden
To be a burden
And above all else
Try your hardest not
To be THE burden
The burden to all but you
Yet you are THE burden
The burden to none but you

Understand

Stop... Feel the book in your hands... its texture... its thickness... its lightweight. It's definitely lighter than the air currently surrounding you.

Wait, maybe not. Extend your arm forward and hold it there... straight forward... absolutely perpendicular to your body with your palm facing upwards. Hold the air... the air that is so weightless... the air that you walk through easily... the air that you inhale... exhale... so easily day in and day out.

Don't put your hand down. I need you to continue to hold the air that is deemed weightless by mankind.

Now understand that this story is about someone you love, care for, and cherish with all of your heart, mind, body, and soul. Somebody that you would sacrifice your own life for if it meant saving theirs. Imagine

their face... water slowly covering their eye, creating a glistening appearance... the water slowly collecting as if it is about to overflow... until the pool reaches its maximum capacity. Each tear begins falling... slowly... ever so gently down their cheek... rolling down their face to be dropped and never seen again.

A burden just like the air. Weightless, while weight filled.

Tears filled with feelings. Full of emotion, too much to hold.

Feel his burden of Support.

<u>Cakes</u>

Cakes – they're gave
They're meticulously made
In Leroy's shop,
That's where memories were made

It didn't matter he was blind
Harbored scoliosis in his spine
Pure care and focus inside
That's what made them sublime

These very cakes support
Birthdays – congrats on sport
Are given to the ones we love
And these lives we support

Yet, emotions – that's what I gave
Unjust, unfair, and unbrave
These emotions so knave
Weren't support, just a grave

A grave to the love you had

And it doesn't even hurt that bad

And honestly – it was all because,

I couldn't even care a tad

But guess what…

**I love me
I love who I am
I love who I was born to be
I love who I was destined to be
I love who I am respectfully**

This is My Burden Of Support

His
Burden Of
Timeliness

Ode Turner

To be the burden

To know a burden
To know how heavy a load things can be
To know how they can affect a person
To know how to deal with a burden

To see a burden
To see what damage it can inflict
To see what unbearable weight drags behind
To see what immense dream can be crushed

To be a burden
To be the creator of turmoil in a life
To be the reason a family has a strife
To be the reason another life has no light

To be the burden
To know a burden
To see a burden
To be a burden
And above all else
Try your hardest not
To be THE burden
The burden to all but you
Yet you are THE burden
The burden to none but you

Understand

Stop... Feel the book in your hands... its texture... its thickness... its lightweight. It's definitely lighter than the air currently surrounding you.

Wait, maybe not. Extend your arm forward and hold it there... straight forward... absolutely perpendicular to your body with your palm facing upwards. Hold the air... the air that is so weightless... the air that you walk through easily... the air that you inhale... exhale... so easily day in and day out.

Don't put your hand down. I need you to continue to hold the air that is deemed weightless by mankind.

Now understand that this story is about someone you love, care for, and cherish with all of your heart, mind, body, and soul. Somebody that you would sacrifice your own life for if it meant saving theirs. Imagine

their face... water slowly covering their eye, creating a glistening appearance... the water slowly collecting as if it is about to overflow... until the pool reaches its maximum capacity. Each tear begins falling... slowly... ever so gently down their cheek... rolling down their face to be dropped and never seen again.

A burden just like the air. Weightless, while weight filled.

Tears filled with feelings. Full of emotion, too much to hold.

Feel his burden of Timeliness.

Tempestuous Time

Part 1

Time… Time… Time…

Funny enough, there's a paradox in every paradigm

Wondering if writing this is even really what I should be doing with my spare time

But ultimately sure that I get enough sleep when it's bedtime

And it's all because of that old cliche, ya' know?

It's, "Health is wealth," right?

So tell me why my schedule continues to be packed tight

Why I ignore myself – working for others as if it's my birthright

Deep down, when I think about it, it may just be out of a refined spite

Spite driven by an unwanted vice from all of those dark nights
Early mornings, accompanied by prolonged and lonely flights
With my mind and perception of self participating in regular fights
Just to put on a smile, prepare for the next match like an armored-knight

And that is my battle with my tempestuous time,
So tell me what you'll do with yours, because I don't know what to do with mine

Part 2

Will it be spent overseas, exploring the Seven Wonders of the World
With you staring in bewilderment at your newfound dreamworld...
Or will it be spent in a house that is not your home

With you begging to escape the place you've always known…

Will it be spent atop the Eiffel Tower with the one that you love
With you staring at the stars, so far, up above…
Or will it be spent working a job that you could never love
With you calling upon your God to save you from so far, up above…

Or it could be none, and you end up caught up in the paradox of time
Looking back at the past-time
   Wishing to relive and steady change the passed time
       Leaving a steady pondering of this paradigm

Part 3

But… I need you to fight against your tempestuous time…
Make your life count while you still have the time
So I ask again…

What will you do with the rest of your time?

Because that is what makes you… You

What you do with your tempestuous time.

But guess what…

I love me
I love who I am
I love who I was born to be
I love who I was destined to be
I love who I am supportingly

This is My Burden Of Timeliness

His
Burden Of
Unerring

Walter Brown

To be the burden

To know a burden
To know how heavy a load things can be
To know how they can affect a person
To know how to deal with a burden

To see a burden
To see what damage it can inflict
To see what unbearable weight drags behind
To see what immense dream can be crushed

To be a burden
To be the creator of turmoil in a life
To be the reason a family has a strife
To be the reason another life has no light

To be the burden
To know a burden
To see a burden
To be a burden
And above all else
Try your hardest not
To be THE burden
The burden to all but you
Yet you are THE burden
The burden to none but you

Understand

Stop... Feel the book in your hands... its texture... its thickness... its lightweight. It's definitely lighter than the air currently surrounding you.

Wait, maybe not. Extend your arm forward and hold it there... straight forward... absolutely perpendicular to your body with your palm facing upwards. Hold the air... the air that is so weightless... the air that you walk through easily... the air that you inhale... exhale... so easily day in and day out.

Don't put your hand down. I need you to continue to hold the air that is deemed weightless by mankind.

Now understand that this story is about someone you love, care for, and cherish with all of your heart, mind, body, and soul. Somebody that you would sacrifice your own life for if it meant saving theirs. Imagine

their face... water slowly covering their eye, creating a glistening appearance... the water slowly collecting as if it is about to overflow... until the pool reaches its maximum capacity. Each tear begins falling... slowly... ever so gently down their cheek... rolling down their face to be dropped and never seen again.

A burden just like the air. Weightless, while weight filled.

Tears filled with feelings. Full of emotion, too much to hold.

Feel his burden of Unerring.

Control's Facade

A magnificent maintenance
Of this fantastic facade
This illusion, this myth
Completely unflawed

Take a walk in my shoes
They're laced; take a stroll
What I speak with my tongue
From the bottom of my soul

Revelations to a prisoner
Control is up to no good
Prisoner's locked away by Control
In a mask and a hood

Prisoner can not lie to a liar
But Control admires a trier
Until Prisoner's free of control
Prisoner can't ascend higher

Steal the keys from Control

Free now in this game we call life

Unblinded from the facade of control

Now, you are truly living life

But guess what…

I love me
I love who I am
I love who I was born to be
I love who I was destined to be
I love who I am timely

This is My Burden Of Unerring

His
Burden Of
Vocation

Aya Ocean

To be the burden

To know a burden
To know how heavy a load things can be
To know how they can affect a person
To know how to deal with a burden

To see a burden
To see what damage it can inflict
To see what unbearable weight drags behind
To see what immense dream can be crushed

To be a burden
To be the creator of turmoil in a life
To be the reason a family has a strife
To be the reason another life has no light

To be the burden
To know a burden
To see a burden
To be a burden
And above all else
Try your hardest not
To be THE burden
The burden to all but you
Yet you are THE burden
The burden to none but you

Understand

Stop... Feel the book in your hands... its texture... its thickness... its lightweight. It's definitely lighter than the air currently surrounding you.

Wait, maybe not. Extend your arm forward and hold it there... straight forward... absolutely perpendicular to your body with your palm facing upwards. Hold the air... the air that is so weightless... the air that you walk through easily... the air that you inhale... exhale... so easily day in and day out.

Don't put your hand down. I need you to continue to hold the air that is deemed weightless by mankind.

Now understand that this story is about someone you love, care for, and cherish with all of your heart, mind, body, and soul. Somebody that you would sacrifice your own life for if it meant saving theirs. Imagine

their face... water slowly covering their eye, creating a glistening appearance... the water slowly collecting as if it is about to overflow... until the pool reaches its maximum capacity. Each tear begins falling... slowly... ever so gently down their cheek... rolling down their face to be dropped and never seen again.

A burden just like the air. Weightless, while weight filled.

Tears filled with feelings. Full of emotion, too much to hold.

Feel his burden of Vocation.

<u>Our Promise</u>

Part 1 - Unwavering Vocational Courage…

Impact steadily questioned inside
Shot down and unappreciated from afar
Receiving absolutely nothing for the credit
Not even enough for a new car

So many countless, untaught lessons
With simply so many more to come
Lives with holes in them, multiplying
Child, please feed your string through some

Know there is value in each of us
Lessons of pain that connect us all
Ponder some, understand the steps
Take some time – retrace them all

Our world's image may remain blurry

All of this tumultuous strife

Sadly, its very essence fading

A pentimento, masking new life

Part 2 - But This Is Our Promise...

A promise to tie a bow

As every life is a gift

Valuing perspectives and heart

Promising not to falter, only lift

Easy? Regretfully not

But let them enjoy your presents

You are truly a wonderful child

Now, share with the world your gift of presence

That Is Our Promise

But guess what…

I love me
I love who I am
I love who I was born to be
I love who I was destined to be
I love who I am unerringly

This is My Burden Of Vocation

His
Burden Of
Wonder

Ejo Ocean

To be the burden

To know a burden

To know how heavy a load things can be
To know how they can affect a person
To know how to deal with a burden

To see a burden

To see what damage it can inflict
To see what unbearable weight drags behind
To see what immense dream can be crushed

To be a burden

To be the creator of turmoil in a life
To be the reason a family has a strife
To be the reason another life has no light

To be the burden

To know a burden
To see a burden
To be a burden
And above all else
Try your hardest not
To be THE burden
The burden to all but you
Yet you are THE burden
The burden to none but you

Understand

Stop... Feel the book in your hands... its texture... its thickness... its lightweight. It's definitely lighter than the air currently surrounding you.

Wait, maybe not. Extend your arm forward and hold it there... straight forward... absolutely perpendicular to your body with your palm facing upwards. Hold the air... the air that is so weightless... the air that you walk through easily... the air that you inhale... exhale... so easily day in and day out.

Don't put your hand down. I need you to continue to hold the air that is deemed weightless by mankind.

Now understand that this story is about someone you love, care for, and cherish with all of your heart, mind, body, and soul. Somebody that you would sacrifice your own life for if it meant saving theirs. Imagine

their face… water slowly covering their eye, creating a glistening appearance… the water slowly collecting as if it is about to overflow… until the pool reaches its maximum capacity. Each tear begins falling… slowly… ever so gently down their cheek… rolling down their face to be dropped and never seen again.

A burden just like the air. Weightless, while weight filled.

Tears filled with feelings. Full of emotion, too much to hold.

Feel his burden of Wonder.

<u>Human Instinct</u>

Our human instinct
We acquire –
We consume –
We take –

Our human instinct
There's more –
There's better –
There's great –

Commercials trigger salivation
In unruly, timely coordination
Perfectly prepared food for thought –
So consume it; Will you not?

Carbonation bubbling across a screen
Bubbles guising as essential
Yet it's simply a fantasy
A fantasy fed to you and me

So, when we have really it all,

Is that when we will truly fall?

You and I, both forced to crawl

Or maybe, that's the end of us all

But guess what…

I love me
I love who I am
I love who I was born to be
I love who I was destined to be
I love who I am vocationally

This is My Burden Of Wonder

His
Burden Of
Xenoglossy

Wayne Martin

To be the burden

To know a burden

To know how heavy a load things can be
To know how they can affect a person
To know how to deal with a burden

To see a burden

To see what damage it can inflict
To see what unbearable weight drags behind
To see what immense dream can be crushed

To be a burden

To be the creator of turmoil in a life
To be the reason a family has a strife
To be the reason another life has no light

To be the burden

To know a burden
To see a burden
To be a burden
And above all else
Try your hardest not
To be THE burden
The burden to all but you
Yet you are THE burden
The burden to none but you

Understand

Stop... Feel the book in your hands... its texture... its thickness... its lightweight. It's definitely lighter than the air currently surrounding you.

Wait, maybe not. Extend your arm forward and hold it there... straight forward... absolutely perpendicular to your body with your palm facing upwards. Hold the air... the air that is so weightless... the air that you walk through easily... the air that you inhale... exhale... so easily day in and day out.

Don't put your hand down. I need you to continue to hold the air that is deemed weightless by mankind.

Now understand that this story is about someone you love, care for, and cherish with all of your heart, mind, body, and soul. Somebody that you would sacrifice your own life for if it meant saving theirs. Imagine

their face... water slowly covering their eye, creating a glistening appearance... the water slowly collecting as if it is about to overflow... until the pool reaches its maximum capacity. Each tear begins falling... slowly... ever so gently down their cheek... rolling down their face to be dropped and never seen again.

A burden just like the air. Weightless, while weight filled.

Tears filled with feelings. Full of emotion, too much to hold.

Feel his burden of Xenoglossy.

Self's Delicacy

Selfless in service –
    genuinely, benevolently
Selfish managing perspectives of you –
    absolutely feverishly

Selfish in controlling –
    never any hesitancy
Selfless in taking the burdens of others –
    sympathetically, empathetically

Selflessness and selfishness,
This dance starts all wars
De capo, again and again,
It's not mine, it is yours

Selfish, greedy need for responsibility –
    completely disreputably
Selfish in credit –
    surely, so incredulously

Selfless in protecting –
    emotionally, definitely
Selfish, in who you protect –
    truly malevolently

Selfishness and selflessness,
This dance starts all wars
De capo, again and again,
It's not mine, it is yours

Encore?

But guess what…

I love me
I love who I am
I love who I was born to be
I love who I was destined to be
I love who I am wonderfully

This is My Burden Of Xenoglossy

His Burden Of Yes

Claire Jenkins

To be the burden

To know a burden
To know how heavy a load things can be
To know how they can affect a person
To know how to deal with a burden

To see a burden
To see what damage it can inflict
To see what unbearable weight drags behind
To see what immense dream can be crushed

To be a burden
To be the creator of turmoil in a life
To be the reason a family has a strife
To be the reason another life has no light

To be the burden
To know a burden
To see a burden
To be a burden
And above all else
Try your hardest not
To be THE burden
The burden to all but you
Yet you are THE burden
The burden to none but you

Understand

Stop... Feel the book in your hands... its texture... its thickness... its lightweight. It's definitely lighter than the air currently surrounding you.

Wait, maybe not. Extend your arm forward and hold it there... straight forward... absolutely perpendicular to your body with your palm facing upwards. Hold the air... the air that is so weightless... the air that you walk through easily... the air that you inhale... exhale... so easily day in and day out.

Don't put your hand down. I need you to continue to hold the air that is deemed weightless by mankind.

Now understand that this story is about someone you love, care for, and cherish with all of your heart, mind, body, and soul. Somebody that you would sacrifice your own life for if it meant saving theirs. Imagine

their face… water slowly covering their eye, creating a glistening appearance… the water slowly collecting as if it is about to overflow… until the pool reaches its maximum capacity. Each tear begins falling… slowly… ever so gently down their cheek… rolling down their face to be dropped and never seen again.

A burden just like the air. Weightless, while weight filled.

Tears filled with feelings. Full of emotion, too much to hold.

Feel his burden of Yes.

Sword Play

Part 1

A shining star in the eyes of them all
We both already know their answer
Steadily spreading your impact and growing
Maybe because you're a cancer

Seemingly, your programmed response
Confidently saying, "Yes, I can sir."
Even before recognizing the request
Seems as if your mind's in a blur

Part 2

I simply want to say to you,

Don't die by the sword that you used to shine
Allow them to then have your head hanging on their shrine

Out there, there are different players, different games

With different motives, different aims

So, attain the very sword you used to shine

Then move forward without a single scar

Because unbeknownst to you, my dear

The light you shine stretches mighty, mighty far

But guess what...

I love me
I love who I am
I love who I was born to be
I love who I was destined to be
I love who I am xenoglossily

This is My Burden Of Yes

His
Burden Of
Zestfulness

Kara Plaid

To be the burden

To know a burden
To know how heavy a load things can be
To know how they can affect a person
To know how to deal with a burden

To see a burden
To see what damage it can inflict
To see what unbearable weight drags behind
To see what immense dream can be crushed

To be a burden
To be the creator of turmoil in a life
To be the reason a family has a strife
To be the reason another life has no light

To be the burden
To know a burden
To see a burden
To be a burden
And above all else
Try your hardest not
To be THE burden
The burden to all but you
Yet you are THE burden
The burden to none but you

Opening

"The generational talent of the GRANDEST instrument… the once child prodigy, now solidified LEGEND in the world of classical music. Welcome to the stage for her FINAL performance for the world, MRS. KARA PLAID," the presenter announces with his booming, deep voice.

The rich, red curtains split in two at the center and roll to their respective sides of the stage, revealing Kara sitting on her chair… the same chair that she has always performed while sitting upon.

This chair is the chair that her brothers gifted to her years ago when she went on her first world tour.

"To Our Precious Sister, From A & P"

That is what is engraved on the long, rectangular, dark silver seat in golden letters.

The audience's cheers begin to grow louder than ever before… and Kara… she is taking this highly emotional and fantastic moment into every depth of her mind and soul.

"Deep breaths, Kara... Deep breaths... Just play again as you always do... Same as if we were just at home alone... just the three of us," she whispers to herself in an effort to relax her nerves.

Although she has always been able to perform without mistake in every single one of her professional performances for over 10 years, she still tends to feel anxiety well up in her system when the curtains reveal her sitting before her absolutely pristine work of art... her music making machine... her beloved organ.

Her instrument is composed of the mahogany body of the device sitting directly in front of her... the mountain of ivory keys, accented by the pitch black keys sitting between every varying number of them... the gorgeous silver and gold pipes lining the stage behind the body of the keyboard... with beautiful, white arches laying atop them as a perfect accentual piece.

"To Our Precious Sister, From A & P," Kara recites before beginning to play an absolute masterpiece of classical work that she created, which is inspired by Johann Pachabel's *Canon in D*. Today was a special day... and those words meant more than they ever did before, so she knew that she had to make today's performance count.

Unbeknownst to the audience, Kara had received a package right before coming on stage... a package that she did not order... a box that she had no recollection of... with no idea where it may have come from.

- Before The Show -

Looking down into her freshly opened cardboard box, she sees a book. A perfect-sized book... not too big... not too small. Not extremely daunting nor underwhelming. She sees the exact book you're reading right now lying perfectly inside the small cardboard box she just opened. Gazing at the cover of this book, she reads, "His Burden Of Zestfulness."

To be exact, right before the curtains revealed the world-class musician, Kara began to read this very book...

Understand

Stop… Feel the book in your hands… its texture… its thickness… its lightweight. It's definitely lighter than the air currently surrounding you.

Wait, maybe not. Extend your arm forward and hold it there… straight forward… absolutely perpendicular to your body with your palm facing upwards. Hold the air… the air that is so weightless… the air that you walk through easily… the air that you inhale… exhale… so easily day in and day out.

Don't put your hand down. I need you to continue to hold the air that is deemed weightless by mankind.

Now understand that this story is about someone you love, care for, and cherish with all of your heart, mind, body, and soul. Somebody that you would sacrifice your own life for if it meant saving theirs. Imagine

their face... water slowly covering their eye, creating a glistening appearance... the water slowly collecting as if it is about to overflow... until the pool reaches its maximum capacity. Each tear begins falling... slowly... ever so gently down their cheek... rolling down their face to be dropped and never seen again.

A burden just like the air. Weightless, while weight filled.

Tears filled with feelings. Full of emotion, too much to hold.

Feel his burden of Zestfulness.

opens book

Kara begins reading…

-

I know we haven't talked in a long time, and it is probably extremely confusing to be reading this from me right now, but I just wanted to reach out to you once again…

So, hey, little sis.

I don't really know how to word this in the right way… or even if there is a "best way" to be writing you at this point in time… but hey.

Right now, I am on an island that I've been making for the past number of years. You already know that the weather is always warm, just as I've always liked, with a beautiful, clean beach with finely ground sand.

I'm writing to you now from my front porch, but I just left the beach from sitting in my dark blue lawn chair… just like the one dad had. You know, the one you and Prince broke that one time.

I miss those days with all of us simply enjoying our family time together… altogether.

I miss the days when you, Prince, and I would all have our mini-concerts at home as if we were performing for the world. You would play your organ, filling our home with beautiful chords… Prince on his cello… and me on my harp. It was an unparalleled and unforeseen trio, but the best trio ever, if I do say so myself.

I miss all of those days…

-

While sitting in her warm-up room, Kara stands up from her chair and begins walking towards the room door. When she reaches the light brown door before her, she grabs the knob, closes it, and locks it before making her way back to her warm-up chair… sitting down before continuing to read.

-

I remember from the day you could walk, you would always try and walk to the grand piano that mom and dad had in the dining room to press the hard white keys with your soft, little, brown hands…

And I don't know what it was about you or what had clicked in your mind when you heard the notes I showed you how to play, but your face would always light up with pure joy and happiness.

And now look at you… from a grand piano in our old family home… all of the way to a grand stage in front of the whole entire world, Kara. I'm so proud of you, and I mean that with everything in me.

The way that you can play rich chords from the C major chord to the A minor chord… blending the notes that you so carefully choose into a perfect harmony using thirds, sixths, and chord progressions… running up and down scales, followed by their arpeggios… it's like magic when you play.

I can see the notes… the high, red notes flying off of the keys as you play… the low, blue notes slowly rising from your fingers as they carry the tone.

Even now, as I listen to your past performances in my current house, I can imagine you playing the songs so elegantly… so joyfully, and full of life.

And the way you play, full of energy, radiates through everyone's minds and souls in the audience... touching their emotions and drawing out the bright side of life, even if just for a moment while you play. That is what makes your music... what makes you unique.

It's not just your music, but also your time and life that is filled with this sort of zest that is genuinely unmatched... untouched... unfathomable really.

You may be my younger sister, but one thing you really have taught me was that I could be my own light in this world. That no matter what is going on in life... no matter how hard I believe that the journey ahead may be... I can still live my best life just like you.

There are so many reasons to get down, try and count myself out each and every day out here, but I just try to think of you. Even though we are so different, I try and think of how you live your life and attempt to replicate it for myself... sometimes though, it is a bit different.

It seems as though I can try and keep this up and maintain this level of energy, but I can't always connect with others in the way you can. Almost as if I am all alone with this love that is meant to be shared.

Can I captivate the world? Sure, I did that with my multimedia empire… I did that with my extensive research and pharmaceutical developments… but what about captivating a soul. How do you captivate a soul?

It has always been something I longed to be able to do… something I have always strived for, and been confused as to why I have never been able to accomplish such a feat.

You have seemed to accomplish this feat on multiple levels from our family, your amazing husband of 4 years, Vic, with the world using your personality and music… but why can't I seem to do this too, Kara? Why not me?

-

Beginning to sob, Kara wipes her eyes… clearing her blurred vision from the tears falling from her light brown eyes…

-

I am steady, a vessel full of zest wanting to share it with everyone, harmonizing and synchronizing with the people I come across… enjoying and cherishing every moment.

Steadily seeking to create a beautiful energy that can be felt altogether.

But then night falls… quiet… each to their own room. Some people are alone… some with their love… some with simply a body… a body to protect them… hold onto through the night, making it as if they aren't truly alone.

However, when the day begins to transform into night… the stars rise. Me… a star sitting alone out in the vast expanse of space… alone… yet shining so brightly as I'm full of desire… thought… joy.

Later, when the night begins to fall… slowly deeper and deeper, I tend to fall… not succumbing to a comfort mechanism of simply having a body… even when the night does fall.

And even when the night envelops the entire sky… I'll pick myself up… full of love, life, and energy, so longing to be shared… noticed by that secret someone. Yet, I shine even brighter as the night goes on… because the darker it gets…, the brighter I shine.

And for that, I thank you… my precious sister… full of zest… life… love… and genuine energy. I thank you for all that you have taught me since the moment you knew how to walk because maybe I'm not meant to share this zest. I could be meant to hold onto it and keep this well running deep inside of me despite what others may think or where I think my energy may need to go. Maybe one day I could find someone to share my well of zest with… or maybe it's just meant for me to hold onto even though I want it to be shared.

Either way, all I know is that I can't be mad at this or hate this fact of my life. I am me, and that is the best I can be… just like you would always tell me, "Just be the best you that you can be, exceptionally."

-

As she reads the last line of the page, her eyes begin to shut as if trying to forget what she had just read.

She opens her eyes, peering through the fog created by her tears, and looks at the same book you're reading right now as she holds it in her right hand. A perfect-sized book… not too big… not too small. Not extremely daunting nor underwhelming. Gazing at the cover of this book, she reads,

But guess what…

I love me
I love who I am
I love who I was born to be
I love who I was destined to be
I love who I am yesfully

This is My Burden Of Zestfulness

The Lost Letters

Unaddressed…

Unassigned…

But A Reason Behind…?

<u>Letter 1</u>

To ...,

I simply wanted to say thank you for helping me cherish my time... Thank you for reminding me to say "I love you" face-to-face each time I leave the presence of someone I love.

In no instance did it feel like the last time you and I would be in poetry club as you taught me how to write limericks... haikus... even acrostics, man. But somehow, there was the last time, and I never saw it coming, and I would hope that you also never saw it coming either.

It's the same as when you, Lane, and I used to play basketball outside of his house. We could have never known that one of those days would be the last time we were all together... us... the trio. It was so joyous the games we played, the memories we made, and the laughs we shared throughout our childhoods. And now look at Lane, man, all of the way to the big stages playing basketball professionally! Now thinking about it, I'd bet we probably had some influence on that, even though we were never as good as him.

But I genuinely appreciate the times that we did have and the impact that you did have on me. I appreciate it because if I had never learned how to enjoy each and every moment… cherish each and every second… I would never be able to truly appreciate every tick on the clock that I spend with the people I love. And for that, I say thank you.

From, A

<u>Letter 2</u>

To …,

Hola… Hello… Bonjour…

The fact that you helped teach me 12 different languages is still, to this day, insane to me. The fact that you've traveled all across the world is even wild to me, even though we traveled most together. I meant to tell you too, but I finally went to Johannesburg, South Africa, a few years ago, and I believe that was my favorite place I've ever been.

However, some things have changed, and I think I need to make a change. I'm not going into it, but I think I've been awoken. Maybe like I've had an "Awakening," you could say… the beginning of something special it seems.

I won't say too much more, but that was my last bonjour.

From, A

<u>Letter 3</u>

To ...,

My beacon of joy and happiness.

I miss you... I miss all of the lively concerts that we went to... the romantic dates that we went on... all of the beautiful memories of our past attempted relationships, really.

I can make any sort of narrative as to why you... why anyone ever came back around. Perhaps it was because I'm at the point I always knew I would be... that I'm doing better than anyone ever thought that I could. Perhaps it was because I have the capability to live and provide a life of the utmost luxury...

Maybe that really is why... but do I care... Actually, no... how can I say I care when I let people walk into my life so easily.

And the thing is, I usually know when someone is lying... I can feel it in my gut...

But especially with the special people that left my life... the ones that keep me thinking of the countless times we had... stomach-hurting laughs we shared... beautiful memories that we made. How can I ever tell them no... how can I ever believe that's their motive.

I deserve so much better than that. That's what I sometimes hear... that I deserve so much better than that... but only the person and I really know what we've shared. How do I ever convince myself otherwise... that it's all a lie... that it's all different now...?

Deep down, I know that may be the case. Deep down, I know that that may very well be reality. And even deeper down... in this endless pit of love in my heart... deep down, I know that there's nothing I can do to stop it.

It sucks because I can be going on the up and up... and then a single text... call... and everything gets thrown off. And why is that? Maybe it's because my soul is attached like I always knew I would be if I ever took that dive.

And I always question why I am like this. Able to let someone in so close... love someone so dearly, and be willing to take a bullet for them... die for them... knowing sure and well that my heart won't run out... the light in my soul won't die out... that my soul's tie won't ever weaken, but steadily get stronger... that each time your tie would be the one to loosen and disappear.

It's crazy, and it sucks... but that's just me and how I am as a person. Especially when it has come to my attempted relationships... fall in... always the last one standing in love... my once companion has gone happily onto the next...

And I don't even hate the person. The person that couldn't compare to the previous... time and time again... Hurting so bad to see you again... think about you again... talk to you again... because I can feel your words... reminisce about our memories... witness your beautiful smile, and hear your oh-so-familiar laugh.

But I love it. It's a craving that surpasses all others... that makes the whole world stop in order to suppress it... but one that I know is worthless and will only end up in me crying... loathing... wishing reality wasn't true.

And yes, of course... I can't be jealous of your next... your next relationship... your friends... or the people that you choose to spend your next block of time with... But I kind of, sort of, am... I wish that it was me, and I wish for nothing in this world.

I still can't be jealous because their moments aren't the same as ours… their smiles aren't the same as ours… their loves aren't the same as ours… so nothing truly compares. So I shouldn't be jealous of them, right? It wouldn't make any sense to… any sense to believe that they can match what we ever had or could have.

But for some reason… maybe I am… hoping someday that it's me again. Me again that you choose over them all. Me again that you want to spend your time with… me again who you want to cherish… me again who you want to be in this world or even another, to the end of time with.

And for some reason… even as I'm writing this now… I still see it in the distance. Maybe it really will be me again… because I continue to have hope that you are my hope… and ask… if you ever did… the answer would be yes.

From, A

If You Always

DREAM & BELIEVE,

You Will Always

GROW & ACHIEVE

~ Jeremiah Pouncy

Made in the USA
Middletown, DE
08 February 2023

24255765R00158